A Girl Called Whisper

Callie Robertson

Printed by Amazon KDP Publishing

Cover Design © 2019 by C.K Robertson
Cover Art © 2019 by Di Dodo Fabio

www.ByCKRobertson.com

For anybody who is struggling.
It will get better.

Callie Robertson

Content Warning: This book contains themes involving alcohol, drugs, sexual abuse, self-harm, and suicide.

CONTENTS

CHAPTER 1

THE MEETING

The rabid screeching of my rooster-imitation phone alarm blasts through my ears and I suffer what I imagine is the equivalent of a mild heart attack. I fumble for my phone on my nightstand and hit snooze, then pull the covers up over my head with a groan.

Mondays are the worst.

Getting up early is the worst.

It's one of my least favourite activities. On the scale of Activities-Cooper-Least-Enjoys-Partaking-In, waking up early comes somewhere between mixed-gender PE classes and holding in a dump you really need to take because you're somewhere inappropriate.

I wish I was a vampire, so I didn't have to sleep. I know vampires aren't real, but for the sake of poetic license, hear me out. I know everybody loves the feeling you get when you slip into your 'warm and inviting' bed at night. You supposedly relax, sigh with relief that the long day is over and fall into a deep and comforting sleep. Well, not me. When I go to bed my head tends to spin around in cycles and ideas and I get stressed out even more than usual because I have nothing else to focus on. It starts small, like thinking about whether something I said earlier sounded stupid, and then it quickly spirals out of control until my gut's clenching and I'm thinking about something dumb I *think* I said to Marie Schooner in 2013.

It always feels like the silence is screaming at me.

Then I wake up in the morning, sweaty, tired and unrested, faced with another long and crappy day that I'll probably stress out about the next night.

I would happily never sleep again if I never had to wake again either. I suppose that's a paradox.

My door swings open, knocking into my dresser beside the doorway as my mum bursts into my room.

"Cooper? For goodness sakes, get out of that damn bed and sort yourself out. You'll miss the bus!" Her voice is a cross between a foghorn and a screaming cat. I wince.

She bats at the duvet as though trying to whack me out of the bed and then she scuttles back out again, muttering about 'lazy godforsaken boys' under her breath. With a sigh, I get out of bed and start to get ready.

I always know to start getting ready when Mum comes to yell at me. This is because she generally waits until approximately 8.20am before coming to wake me up herself, fuelled by the fear that she will miss the start of *The Morning Show* to drive me into school if I miss the bus.

By 8.20am I have twenty minutes to get showered, dressed, and eat my breakfast before having to leave for the bus. I can shower in five, dress in ten and eat in five. I have perfected the routine down to the last second.

I like to invest a little more time into dressing, because I feel better during the day if I know I'm 'fitting in.'

There are three types of kids at my school who get the most shit: the ones who are socially inept, the ones who *look* socially inept, and the ones who are both.

I have accepted the fact that I struggle more than most people in social situations. Probably because I like to avoid them altogether. I have an extensive vocabulary (which I do try to dumb down in all fairness,) and an unaccommodating distrust of my fellow classmates. These personality factors make me a tasty target for bullying; a juicy young deer thrown amidst a ravenous pack of well-dressed and poorly-spoken wolves.

Dressing to blend in and avoid attracting unwanted attention makes me feel more at ease. It seems to work, too.

It's a pretty simple algorithm really: I take into account what seems to be trending, make sure I'm wearing it, and keep myself to my damn self. The current 'cool trend' are these mini backpacks from the sports store in town. They look ridiculous and aren't even large enough to be practical for school, but everyone else was getting them, so I got one too. And I saw a kid with a briefcase-style book bag getting food thrown at him yesterday in the canteen, so it just goes to show really. (Of course, there are a plethora of reasons that John Everist may have been the target of the food-throwing, his bag being only one potential motive. Rather him than me; it's a dog-eat-dog world out there.)

Today I opt for some inconspicuous black jeans, a white polo-neck shirt which is a bit big for me, but they didn't have it in my size, and the stupid mini backpack. For the record, I am an uninteresting size S. Not quite man enough to reach M, yet not quite measly enough to be XS. Silver linings, my friend.

I put on my generic Nike trainers and head down to breakfast.

Every morning I have toast with Marmite on it. I don't know why, I just really, really like Marmite. Enough to have it every morning of my life and not get bored. Also, if I'm running late, I can spread it super quickly and just run out of the door, toast in mouth, though Mum nags about me doing this. She thinks it's rude to not sit down for five minutes with the family every morning. My family aren't the most exciting people on the planet, so if I do skip breakfast, I don't feel too bad about it. I doubt I miss out on any jaw-dropping, life-changing conversation. No cures for cancer or global warming solutions will be lost on me.

My sister is already at the table. She's four years older than me - twenty. She has long dark hair and big brown eyes and her name is Bella, which means 'beautiful' in Italian. My sister *is* beautiful, and all the boys in my class fancy her. I'm not sure how I feel about this. On one hand, it's gross, and I hate hearing them say vulgar things about her. On the other hand, I get a lot less shit in my day-to-day life because they somehow respect me for having a hot older sister. It makes no sense, but I don't dispute it. If having an attractive older sibling somehow gets me higher on the social ladder than poor old John Everist, I'll take it.

I get on well with my sister, but we don't really hang out together. This suits me, because her friends aren't the type of people I'd choose to spend my time with.

The boys all look a little like well-groomed aliens with a shit-ton of gel in their hair and the girls all use abbreviated words, which makes me embarrassed to even listen to. Even Bella speaks like that when she's around them, though she drops the act when it's just us at home.

They make me feel uncomfortable as I'm not sure how to speak to them and I feel like I don't belong. This makes me sweat. You will notice sweating is a frequent occurrence in my miserable life, and it's boring and gross but it's part of who I am and as long as I keep wearing deodorant it's not like it's hurting anybody. For the record, I use the 48-hour dry protection stuff. And yes, I have a can in my mini backpack, alongside my anxiety tablets and whatever sandwich Mum stuffs in there for the day. Dad says it's all down to hormones, but I know it's to do with my feeling uncomfortable. I let him think it's hormones. He says it all proud, as if he's finally getting his very own, size Small, man-child.

Back to my sister and away from my body malfunctions: Bella is a hairdresser, but she's doing a degree in Psychology part-time. This makes her think she has the right to psychoanalyse me on a daily basis.

While I eat my toast, I can hear the dance music coming out of her headphones, her hair wild and unruly underneath it. She bops her head to the music and eats her muesli. She loves her muesli, says it's good for you. I think it looks like bird food. She says it will help her to lose weight, which I don't understand either because she doesn't need to lose any. Dad says all women want to lose weight, and even if they don't, they say they do anyway. I don't really understand this. I don't understand most other people anyway, but girls' heads are even more complicated to figure out. Dad says it's not worth even trying.

I also don't understand how it's not okay for me to grab my toast for an on-the-run breakfast because I should be 'spending time with the family', but Bella can stick headphones in and not speak to any of us and that is somehow acceptable. I bring this up a lot with Mum, but she doesn't do much about it. Bella says me acting up about her breakfast ritual is my insecurity complex flaring up, because she is the girl of the family and therefore more likely to be favoured. This is one of many examples of Bella's Bullshit Brain-Analysis.

I finish my breakfast and say goodbye.

Bella says 'laters' and Mum kisses me on the forehead and says what she always does, "Have a lovely day, make good choices and be happy."

Dad looks up from his paper. "Bye, champ."

The same as any other goddamn day. My life is a series of unstimulating events.

I walk down to the bus stop, the rows of uninteresting same-same suburban houses passing me by. The postman, Steve, waves at me and I nod back. It's a nice sunny day, and there's a crisp freshness in the air.

"Get off. Hey, stop!"

My attention's broken and across the street I see one of the Posh Twats from the other school in our town. His bag's been thrown on the floor and a couple of kids I recognise from my own school are laughing and kicking it while he tries to pick up his books. I feel bad for him, but keep my head down and my eyes to the floor. Like I said before, it's a dog-eat-dog world and at this stage I'd rather it was him than me. My pace picks up slightly and I hurry towards my

—

bus stop. I don't want to draw attention to myself, and luckily for me, I blend in nicely. Unlucky for him, he doesn't. The kids from Posh Twat School (PTS) have to wear uniforms. Fancy-ass blazers and ties and even a goddamn crest-embroidered book bag, can you believe? It just makes them easy targets. One time, one of the after-school fights got so huge that police were called and had to break it up, they turned up in riot vans and everything. It was all anybody was talking about the next day. Obviously I don't partake in these tussles, just hear about them. Why would anybody want to spend any time with people in town after school has ended? I like to live vicariously through overheard snippets of conversation from everyone else. I glance back and see the boy scowling, his blazer crumpled and his rucksack swung back across his shoulder. The boys from my school saunter off, slapping each other's backs and jeering. I shoot him a remorseful nod, but I don't think he notices.

When I reach my stop, I stand on my own and wait for the bus while everyone else stands in their groups of friends, catching up on their weekends. I don't have any proper friends at my school. My best friend is Harry, who used to live next door to me. His family moved to the other side of town now and up-sized to a detached house. We've known each other since we were really small - a penchant for catching bugs in jars brought us together. Fortunately we grew out of that hobby quite quickly. He goes to PTS, which has led to his being christened with the nickname The Prince. Plus, he coincidentally shares a first name with Britain's favoured royal, so it makes sense from all angles. I see Prince a lot, but times like this I wish he went to my school so I had someone to chat with while I wait. Instead I put my headphones in and lean against a small brick wall, staring at my feet as I listen to the clash of *Wolfmother*.

Everyone at my school is into commonly 'cool' things, like football and hip-hop. I like to paint and read, so I don't really fit in. I actually applied to go to PTS, but they were oversubscribed. Most likely with all the other uncool people from Bennesons (my school) who, like me, are trying to climb their way into some sort of social spotlight in an alternative educational environment. Imagine a world where brains won over brawns? Fantasy.

Mum even wanted to send me to a goddamn 'special school' for a while, because she thought my struggles to fit in were worsening my diagnosed anxiety. Can you believe that? Being on the special bus is the last goddamn thing I need.

After that horrendous suggestion I made a conscious effort to fit in better and to stop talking about the things that worry me. Since doing so, alongside taking my prescribed medication, I haven't felt half as anxious as I did before. Placebo effect? Perhaps.

Dad's on my side too. "There's nothing wrong with my boy, he's a great lad and everybody should stop fussing and leave him be," he said.

So Mum left me to be.

I'm just a bit socially awkward, that's all. Prefer my own company. Introverted. No big deal.

The bus arrives and I wait for everybody else to board first before getting on and taking my usual seat at the very front with the bus driver, Marvin. He's pretty old, with wiry grey hair and loads of face wrinkles but he's always smiling and

I've seen him shaking his fist at bad drivers so he's still got a bit of a spark about him.

"Good morning, Marvin."

"Good day! How are we, young Cooper?" he asks back jovially.

"Alright," I reply.

Marvin nods and off we go.

I always sit at the front because when I sat elsewhere, the other kids used to give me trouble. This was a long time ago, when I first came to Bennessons, but they called me names and pulled at my clothes and antagonised me into fights. One time I got really angry and hit this boy, Blake, because he was calling me a retard. That fight was in my first week of Bennessons when I was eleven. I've sat here, with Marvin, ever since.

I like to use the bus journey to read, anyway. Usually I don't read in public as part of my method for fitting in, but when I sit at the front with Marvin everyone acts like I'm not here. This suits me fine, because I can read in peace and nobody gives me any shit for it. Also, if something great happens in the storyline, I tell Marvin about it and he nods and asks questions, which I like. I always read fantasy novels. They're usually fat and bulky and take up a lot of precious mini-backpack space, but I love how anything can happen in these worlds. Magic and apocalypses and crazy shit. I think it's cool, like whoever has written it has bent the rules of the world to create something totally new. When I'm reading it's like I can envision it all happening in my head so clearly, sometimes I go back home and recreate scenes as drawings.

We arrive at school and I wait for everybody to get off before I do, ears pricking up and catching slithers of conversation as people bustle past me in a tirade of mid-conversations.

"And then she told him no way- "

"She was like, amazing, and he was like, isn't it? And -"

"So then I looked in the toilet and this dump was freaking huge man, like-"

"I swear my Mum is the biggest bitch I've ever -"

I swing my dumb backpack onto my shoulder, grab my folders and shuffle off, giving Marvin a nod of departure.

"See you on the way home," he waves and pulls away, the door closing after me. He's a good guy.

I turn to face the dreaded doors of Bennesson and sigh, trying to pump myself up for the day. The Dreaded Doors of Bennesson - that would be a great book name. I should log that somewhere. Everybody around me is chatting excitedly as they enter the school, exchanging gossip and sharing uninteresting opinions about reality TV shows I don't watch. The building looms up into the sky and looks... depressing. Grey and bleak and depressing. Inside isn't much better, gross green plastic-like flooring and fluorescent lights that, I'm sure, were designed specifically to highlight sixteen-year-old-boy's pimples as brightly as possible.

On cue, the bell screams and there is a collective groan as everybody starts hustling towards class, lockers slamming and footsteps padding down the halls.

I don't have first period today. I get to miss my first class to go and see Suzie, the guidance counsellor. I have a private session with her twice a month, which is great for getting me out of class.

I wait outside her office and try not to jiggle my knee. I'm not sure what I'll talk about today and feel uncomfortable going in without a set plan. I like plans.

Her office is beside the Head Teacher, Mr Gray's office. Opposite me sits Miles Jenson, one of the more popular kids at school. He's sat with his legs spread wide, slumped into a chair with his arms crossed and a scowl on his face, a hood hanging low over his forehead. He looks like he'll stab me if I disturb him. I try to avoid eye contact, but I can feel his eyes boring into me and it makes my pulse quicken.

I glance quickly to the side and clench and unclench my fists. My knuckles crack.

Mr Gray's door swings open. "Come in, Jenson. And pull those blooming trousers up, for Christ's sake!"

I watch as Miles trudges up and follows Mr Gray into his office, the door shutting behind him, and let out a small sigh of relief. No altercation after all.

"Come on in, Cooper!" Suzie's head pops around the door a moment later and I get up and trail into her office. It's small and painted yellow, a bunch of Thank You cards line her desk from parents and students. She smells of soap and has really long, red wavy hair. Her voice is really gentle and lullaby-esque, so when she speaks everything else around me somehow gets quiet, my insides feel still and my head calms down. She smiles and sits down at her desk, looking at me expectantly. She always waits for me to start the conversation, I learnt this pretty early on when we spent our first session together in silence for the first fifteen minutes.

I see Suzie for my anxiety disorder. It's not a learning difficulty - I'm of above-average intelligence for my age group. My anxiety just makes it a little harder for me in certain social situations, which in turn makes me less confident, which makes me more anxious. It's a raging cycle of useless behavioural patterns. Suzie helps with this sort of thing. I don't necessarily have to see her every fortnight now that I have my panic attacks under control, but I like to keep going anyway because it gets me out of class for an hour.

Kids go to see her for loads of different reasons; when their parents are divorcing, if they're hurting themselves, if they're too thin, if they're bullying people... the list is extensive. Sometimes they are forced to go by Mr Gray, as punishment for something, but usually they go by choice. She's helped so many kids with family problems that there's an unspoken respect for her and anybody who needs to speak to her to deal with stuff. If anyone asks why I'm going to see her, I make a conscious effort to look very sullen and say, 'family issues' and then the person asking will look empathetic and nod. It's the unspoken rule at Bennesson's: nobody gets crap for seeing Suzie, because she's the goddamn nicest woman to live on this earth.

I like my time with Suzie. I show her sketches I'm working on and talk about books I've read. She likes my paintings a lot, so sometimes I do special ones just for her when I'm feeling nice. I don't make a habit of it or anything. In return for my paintings, she gives me book recommendation lists which she thinks I will enjoy. It's like having a friend at my school, only she's way older than me and I can only speak to her twice monthly. I don't want it to get weird and her to think I fancy her or anything. Christ, *imagine*.

We go over coping mechanisms for anxiety, and I talk to her about anything causing me particular stress at the time.

Today nothing is particularly bothering me, but I need time to drag out because my first class is Math which I really don't excel in, so I want to miss as much as possible. I'll have to pull something good out of the bag. *Out of the bag...*

"My bag is stressing me out." I tell her, my face sombre.

She glances quickly at my bag, which is sat by my feet. I kick it to emphasise my distaste.

"Why is your bag stressing you out, Cooper?" she asks me with her baby-voice. She says my name a lot. I think she does this to feel like she is connecting with me and to encourage me to open up more.

"It's not big enough for my folders." I hold up my folder to magnify the severity of the situation, "which means I have to carry them, in which case I may as well not even have a bag and just carry all my stuff into school by hand like a stockroom assistant."

She nods slowly. I can't tell if she's humouring me or not, so I carry on, feeling like I'm on a bit of a roll.

"It cost me seventeen quid down at Sports Bucket and it probably cost an overseas factory worker about twenty pence to make. It's a daily reminder of my conformist attitude and I hate it." I glare at the bag to make my point.

"So why don't you buy another bag?" Suzie asks. It took her two minutes of listening to my made-up rant before asking me this, the most obvious question. Suzie is a good listener.

"Because I'll get beaten up," I announce, feigning exasperation.

Sudden inspiration hits and I begin to improvise a speech Mr Luther King would be proud of.

"Some kid the other day with a briefcase big enough to fit all his folders, and probably mine too, got Baked Beans thrown at him at lunchtime. Of the Heinz variety," I add, as though it makes a difference. "You think that's a coincidence, Suzie? Because I sure as hell don't. So here I am, paying my seventeen quid and being a sell-out because society is telling me that if I buy an appropriate and sensible school bag, I'll get Beaned." I pause, impressed by my use of the word 'beaned' as a verb.

"Who got Baked Beans thrown at him?" Suzie asks sharply, snapping to attention.

I fold my arms. "Snitches get stitches," I reply.

I sit and half-listen to Suzie give an empowering speech about being myself and spending my money on things I want to buy without caring what other people think. She tells me anybody who gives me trouble can be reported in confidence and they'll get their just comeuppance. Yeah, and so would I. *Snitches get stitches,* I think to myself.

"What about when you leave school? Will you still have this bag?" she asks me, batting her big blue eyes at me curiously. I blink. I wasn't expecting this. After I leave school… part of me thinks I'll finally be free to be myself and stop caring what other people think of me. But the other half of me is terrified. "I…I don't know," I stammer out eventually.

"Do you *want* to have this bag?" Suzie asks, watching me carefully.

"No," I reply straight away. "But I don't know where I'll be."

"What difference does that make?"

I swallow. "Well, I'm hoping I'll get into art school in the city," I explain slowly. Suzie nods along supportively. "And in my head art school will be full of people like me and I won't need a Conformist Bag. But just thinking about college freaks me out. What if I don't get in? What if I *do* get in? Is that my whole life planned out? What if I get in, but I'm still not good enough? What if I get in and it's the exact same as school, except everyone is great at art and not just me?"

I would lose myself. Being good at art is all I have to distinguish myself from everyone at this school. If I'm just one small fish in a big pond of arty fish, who am I? I clench my fists.

"It's all so unknown. I'd have to socialise with all new people, blend in amongst people who have the same interests as me but might be better. Maybe these backpacks won't be cool there, and they'll all see right through me for being such a conformist." I know I'm babbling, but I can't help it, and Suzie says nothing, so I carry on.

"What if everyone hates me? Or I find out I'm actually terrible at art compared to other people and I'm stuck at college for three years being known as a failure? Surely that's worse than not getting in at all?"

Suzie shrugs calmly. "Is that really what you think?"

"I don't know!" I choke out. How did this conversation turn around so quickly? I was fine when I came in, and now I'm definitely not.

The bell rings for English. *No.* It's too soon. I'm too stressed.

"If you're feeling okay you can go now, Cooper. I'll see you in a fortnight and we'll pick these college concerns back up.

There's clearly a lot to discuss." She smiles at me and I pick up my Conformist Backpack. I'm flustered, I'm afraid, and on top of all that, I'm going to be late.

I walk in after everybody else has sat down, clenching and unclenching my fists as I feel the teacher pause mid-sentence to look at me, The Late Arrival. I'm sure everybody is looking at me, laughing inside, but I stare fixedly at the floor. That's when I notice a pair of battered lace-up boots. There is a girl I don't know standing at the front of the class with our teacher and she looks over at me with her big blue eyes and I feel myself get hot. This means I'm probably going red, for which I loathe myself. I want to jump into a lake of starved crocodiles, hungry for my not-very-meaty-half-pubescent body.

"Sit down, Cooper. You're late." Mrs Hadlow gestures to a seat, peering at me with a look of contempt over her glasses. She turns back to address the room. "I was just about to introduce your new classmate."

I shuffle over to my desk, my face burning.

"Everybody, this is Whisper, she has moved from London to join us. I hope you will make her feel welcome," she continues.

The class snigger at the girl's name and she stands there steely still, glaring out into the room with a slight pout.

I don't snigger, despite my usual intention to follow the crowd. I like her name, it's different - like her.

She is the most beautiful girl I have ever seen.

Her hair is metallic black and short, scraped up in a messy and stubby ponytail. She's wearing red lipstick which makes her look so much older and more sophisticated than the other girls in the class. Her cheeks are rosy and she's wearing a ton of black eye makeup, that make her blue eyes look even colder as she glares out into the room.

She has a tiny nose stud that sparkles when light catches it and her nails are bitten down to nubs, but she's painted them with black nail varnish, so they still look fascinating somehow. Her skirt is hitched right up, so I can see a scab on her knee, and her jumper is tight against her curves, which makes me hot again when I realise I'm staring. If she's a whisper, I'm deathly silence.

Our teacher tells her she can take a seat and Whisper stalks over to the last free chair, two rows along from mine. Her boots squeak on the linoleum floor. She slumps over her table chewing strawberry bubblegum that must be fresh out of the packet, as I can smell it from where I'm sat.

She fiddles with her pen, weaving it around her fingers and stopping to doodle flowers and stars on her notebook sporadically. I watch her as she writes 'Whisper' in swirly, cursive writing over and over again at the top of the page. It reads like goddamn poetry.

CHAPTER 2

FLIRTING 101

I spend the majority of my time during the class trying to look at Whisper without making it obvious I'm doing so. She's in her own world of doodled flowers and under-the-desk texting and barely notices anything going on around her. I'm not the only one intrigued by her. I see girls looking her up and down, whispering and passing notes to each other. Boys eye her greedily as well, talking loudly and showing off for her attention, trying to make a lasting impression. I blend into the background as usual. Cooper Nobody Nelson.

I don't want to blend in today though, I want her to notice me.

The bell rings to signal the end of class and for once, I'm feeling... confident? Excited? Determined? Whatever it is, it's a foreign feeling, but I feel it nonetheless. I feel like a new person, like my determination to be noticed is overriding all my typical personality traits. Is this what it's like for animals, when natural instinct kicks in if a potential mate is nearby? About time my hormones actually made an appearance. My chest puffs out slightly and my hands remain by my sides, unclenched, though the tips of my fingers curl. I want to speak to Whisper. I don't want to be a nobody today. Something about her draws me in, like a painting I can't figure out. I don't care if I leave Bennessons and nobody ever remembers me, but I want her to be the exception.

What if she hates me? What if she laughs at me? What if everyone else laughs at me? What if my top is too plain for her? What if she's more of a v-neck kind of girl? I shake my head to myself - I would never wear a goddamn v-neck.

I start to feel skittish and my fingers itch to curl. Deep breaths. She's new, she doesn't know anybody - now is my best chance. Before she realises what a nomad I am. I'd never usually do something like this, but it feels like it's now or never. I push my worries to the side and decide that the best plan of action will be to introduce myself to her, and to do it quickly before I lose my nerve.

I'm walking behind her, trying to work out what to say. I never usually speak to people first. Christ, I hope I don't start sweating.

She has a strange gait, like a newborn, gangly deer. All limbs jutting out at awkward angles. I'm inspecting her knees with mild fascination when she turns around. Shit.

"I'm Cooper Nelson," I splutter quickly. I stick out my hand for a handshake and realise instantly that it's too formal. Hopefully she'll just think I'm more sophisticated than our idiot classmate counterparts. Or she might think I'm a sixty-year-old CEO trapped in a sixteen-year-old's body. It's a gamble. I curse myself in my head and know that I will spend approximately the next six years hating myself for this exact moment every time I close my eyes to go to sleep. Why did I have to go and stick out my goddamn hand?

After what feels like an hour of standing there like an idiot she smiles and grabs my hand.

It feels electric. I almost physically sag in relief.

"Whisper." She introduces herself with a handshake that's confident and strong. Dad always says a solid handshake signifies a powerful person. Whisper is definitely that, I can tell already. She doesn't even have a (mentioned) second name, like Madonna or Cher or something. Her fingers are laden with big chunky rings, like a knuckle duster made of jewels.

"Do you have any pets?" I quickly ask, in an attempt to keep conversation flowing. It was the first thing I thought of that I was certain didn't come across like I was a serial killer or a rapist. Also, who doesn't like animals? Even the mere mention of animals should illustrate myself as a caring and sentimental young man.

She looks a bit confused. "No... I wish I did though. I had a goldfish when I was a kid, called Rupert. He died." Her voice is gritty like when you have a sore throat.

I swallow reflexively.

"I have a dog called Max. He isn't dead yet." I inform her. "Max is a Basset Hound. He looks constantly depressed; I occasionally fear he may be mildly suicidal," I add.

She peers at me oddly for a minute, squinting her eyes at me as though trying to work something out. Then she snaps back up to attention. "Well, I'd love to meet him one day."

The bell rings and she flashes me one more smile with her ridiculously white teeth (I should ask her for her orthodontist, there is no way her teeth can be so naturally perfect) and hurries away down the hall again, her knees sticking out slightly. If she wants to meet Max, she would have to come to my house. The thought of her ever being remotely near my house both terrifies me and excites me. Mostly terrifies.

My next class is art, which is obviously one of my favourites and I chose it specifically. It doesn't even really feel like a lesson because I just sit and draw which is basically what I do the whole time I'm at home. Even the smell of chalk and paint as I walk in is calming. Not that I'm sniffing paint fumes. I'm not, the whole room just smells of paint. Besides, I'm pretty sure they use the non-toxic acrylic stuff here because a kid squirted a tube up his nose once and had to go to hospital. See what I mean about moronic classmates?

I trail into the room with everyone else and straight away notice that Whisper isn't here, which means she must have chosen to take music class instead. I'm slightly disappointed, but at least I can concentrate on my work without her around to distract me. I'd like to pretend I'm mature enough not to let a girl throw me off, but English class already proved that theory wrong. Clearly I do have hormones after all - Dad would be so pleased to know.

Today we're painting in the style of the artist we have chosen for our final project. The artist I chose is Damien Vent. He's a really cool graphic illustrator who focuses on portraits of people, mostly black and white but then he adds splashes of colour, which makes it look more modern. He has pop-art influences in his work and always puts in loads of detail, making them more hyper-realistic. I chose him because he does a lot of comic work and he illustrated a fantasy novel I read ages ago called Death After Life. The book was terrible, but I always remembered the cover. It was this woman who was basically strangling herself with her own hair, but she was painted so beautifully and there were splashes of red everywhere to look like blood. I'm not into gore or anything, but it was a bold look and I can appreciate that.

My final project for the year will be to create a huge piece based on Damien's work and a project book full of research. (Written and drawn.)

Today I'm painting an angel, with black hair that touches the floor, blood red lips, and fingers laden with sparkling rings. I ink her in carefully and give her a golden shining halo and white jagged wings that look like they've been ripped at with a knife. True artists draw inspiration from their real lives, and I undoubtedly drew some inspiration from this morning's interactions. Not like Whisper's becoming my muse or anything, that would be weird. I always try to let the world around me inspire my work, so I'm acting like this is just a normal, everyday painting. But it's not. It feels different - special somehow. I'm embarrassed by how much she's affected me, but I can't seem to shake this fascination I have about her. Besides, it's one of the best things I've created recently.

My art teacher, Mr Thomas, walks behind me and inspects it. "Absolutely fantastic work, Cooper. Really good use of contrast shading."

He walks on and I hear someone whisper 'faggot' at me.

I pretend I didn't hear.

As soon as I get home, I text Prince. We text pretty much every day, just to keep each other in the loop with what's going on. (Spoiler: usually, nothing.) But today is different.

Today I met a girl that I may be interested in actually speaking to, which I don't think has ever happened before. This is big news in our world, and I'm hoping Prince can give me some encouragement and words of wisdom. He was actually the one who got me into drawing in the first place. We were eight, and I was having my first panic attack. He freaked out and didn't know what to do whilst I hyperventilated in his bedroom. He thrust a colouring book and crayons into my face and the two of us coloured in until I had calmed down again, and I've been drawing ever since. He probably doesn't even remember it. He always knows what to do, even without realising.

- Come over ASAP!

I add the exclamation point and a couple of firework emojis for good measure, to emphasise the urgency of the situation. He turns up twenty minutes later, his beaten up old Ford chugging onto my driveway loudly.

I listen to him stampede up the stairs and seconds later he bursts through the door, launching himself onto my bed where he lays back and immediately pulls out a bag of skins from his pocket and begins rolling a cigarette. Prince is not allowed to smoke, so he does so in my house, because Dad wouldn't notice if Prince asked him to borrow a lighter and Mum pretends it's not happening as long as he does it out the window.

Prince has shaggy brown hair which he wears messy (like all the PTS students) and wears glasses. He is substantially broader than me having endured an enviable growth spurt last summer. His hands work at the paper like second nature as he walks over and leans out of the window, lighter in hand.

"What's up then? Two emojis seems excessive, for you."
He raises an eyebrow, smoke billowing out of his mouth. I
try not to grimace at the smell.

"I met a girl."

"So? I meet tons of girls every day." He shrugs his (now
size M/L, previously-last-summer size S) shoulders with a
smirk.

"Not one that I possibly want to actually speak to. As in, on
a regular basis," I explain, feeling a bit stupid. "I could do
with some help in the whole speaking-to-girls department."

He peers at me whilst picking a spot on the side of his face
and I can practically hear the cogs working in his head as he
tries to figure out what sage advice to give me.

The thing is, I'm pretty sure that despite his epic tales of
private school debauchery and changing-room orgies,
Prince is as useless at girls as I am. I mean, I've never
actually *seen* him with a girl before.

"Let's Google chat up lines." My suspicions are confirmed.

I get the laptop out and we are instantly bombarded with
the biggest load of shit that I have ever read.

"You are almost as beautiful as my twin sister, but that's
illegal," I read out in disbelief.

"Don't say that to her, for the love of God. Although your
sister is *sa-moking*," Prince licks his lips and I groan before
punching him lightly on the shoulder.

"I'm no Fred Flinstone, but I could make your bed rock.
That's the one, Cooper. Winner, winner, chicken dinner!" he
fist-pumps the air.

I doubt I could make her bed even slightly wobble, let
alone rock. "This is useless. Let's just give up, accept our
losses and get some pizza."

Prince shrugs.

He sticks around for a while more and starts watching porn in fascination (another thing he won't do in his house but will besmirch my own home with) while I lie on my bed thinking about when I'm going to quit being a wimp and talk to her again. In the hallway? Before class? No, after class. Gives me something to talk about. I could make a witty joke about how boring and lame it was.

"So," Prince starts, finally peeling himself away from his depraved phone screen, "when are you seeing her next?"

"I guess we'll have class together again tomorrow. I haven't worked out what subjects she's chosen yet."

"You know, man, I'm proud of you," he tells me with a small nod.

"Proud of me?"

"Yeah, you spoke to her. Introduced yourself and everything. You never act like that usually, it's a big deal and you should be happy with yourself. She knows who you are, so now she can't ignore you without looking like a rude bitch. And if she does, that's not the type of girl you want anyway."

He turns back to his screen which is moaning increasingly loudly and I smile to myself. He's a goddamn idiot, but he somehow says the right thing when I need to hear it.

So, my alarm is going off and - get this - I get up straight away.

After Prince left I was feeling positive about the girl situation and I'm ready to tackle the day and see Whisper again, this time without the knee-staring and goddamn hand-shaking.

I get ready and hell, does Mum look shocked when I stroll down the stairs dressed and on time. I have to push my tongue to the roof of my mouth to stop from laughing at her expression. She looks like someone's invited her onto The Morning Show to talk about her five favourite cleaning products. Seeing as I woke up straight away and have extra time to kill, I offer to help with breakfast and she steps back, eyeing me suspiciously like I'm a 99% off discount voucher.

"Alright, I give. What's going on? What's the catch?" She folds her arms as though I'm tricking her.

I ignore her and spread my Marmite. It slaps and squelches satisfyingly.

"Is something special happening at school today?" she tries again.

My mouth tilts into an upwards curve and I know I'm about to cave. I rarely break my don't-tell-Mum-shit rule, but I'm excited and want to speak to someone other than Prince about Whisper. "I met a girl yesterday. I think she might become a new friend," I add quickly when I see Mum go pink. 'I met a girl yesterday' probably translates into 'I got a girl pregnant yesterday' to my mother. I wouldn't be surprised if I came home to my room filled with condoms and teenage pregnancy statistics printed on the walls.

Little does she know, I am at the bottom of all social ladders and my chances of ever impregnating any woman are slim to nil. For starters, I would have to take one on a date first. Which would involve asking someone on a date. Which I have no intention of doing - I'm still riding the glory of merely sharing my name with a female.

I instantly regret involving Mum as she starts bombarding me with questions that I have no answers to. Questions about Whisper's parents, her classes, her likes and dislikes. "Mum, I don't know anything about her! Except that she would like a dog." I add as an afterthought. I don't tell her about the nose piercing. Mum nods, but she understands nothing.

"Well, if you asked her out on a little date, that would be the perfect chance to find out all about her," she says breezily, as though casually asking someone as beautiful as Whisper on a date is something I would be able to do. I roll my eyes and she catches me.

"I'm serious, Cooper! When your father asked me out he took me to the fish and chip shop, I ordered chicken and he made fun of me the entire time for it. 'Who goes to the fish and chip shop for chicken?' he would say. Anyway, we laughed the entire time and by the time the date was over I knew the most important thing about him. That we had the same sense of humour." She smiles at me knowingly.

"Who goes on a first date to a fish and chip shop?" Bella shouts from the living room with a snort.

Mum goes red. "In my day it was different. There weren't all these fancy restaurants in the town where we grew up, you took what you could get!"

"That's what Dad was doing," Bella cackles.

"Bella, you watch that dirty mouth of yours!" Mum gasps, leaning into the living room to lecture her. I take the opportunity to forget breakfast and sneak out. There are few ways I enjoy spending my mornings, but listening to Bella being a wind-up and Mum lecturing her is not one of them.

I think about the questions Mum asked on the way to the bus stop. I want to know all about Whisper, her ins and outs. I've known her for less than 24 hours and am already consumed with a desire to know more about her. What makes her tick, what her favourite food is, what music makes her sad, what movies make her happy... this is probably bad news.

If this was a teenage rom-com, this would be the part where the music kicks in to let you know a tricky situation is about to ensue. Unfortunately, it's not a blockbuster, just my pathetic life.

"Good morning, young Cooper," Marvin chirps at me as I board the bus.

"Good morning, old Marvin," I respond. Cheeky, I know.

"How are we today?"

"Good today, Marv. I'm feeling pretty damn good today. I'm kind of making friends with this girl. Her name is Whisper – weird name, I know." I explain. I feel so empowered by the fact that I actually approached someone and introduced myself - it makes me want to yell it from the rooftops. I want to share my news with anyone that will listen, so they know that I'm a little bit cooler than they might have thought before.

"My wife was called Fontaine. She knew all about strange names," he replies with a chortle. "Let me tell you something. The weird ones are always the best ones," he gives me a cheeky grin as I sit down.

"Keep me up to date with your shenanigans," he adds as he shifts into gear.

"I will, though I can't promise there will be much to tell," I admit with a shaky laugh.

My fists clench and unclench clammily. I don't bother reading for the rest of the journey, even though I have to get through another chapter of Frankenstein for English class. I'm getting nervous at the prospect of today, of seeing Whisper and working out what to say. My stomach feels like I might barf everywhere.

This kid, who was unfortunately nicknamed Barfy Ben, threw up on the bus a few years ago from travel sickness and now he has to sit on his own every day. The alliteration in his nickname is unfortunate – if it wasn't so damn catchy, I'm sure it wouldn't have stuck with him for this long.

I can't remember the last time I got excited about seeing someone, or felt like I had met somebody who had the potential of actually becoming a friend. I can't even remember when I met Prince. I think I just saw him in the garden and we just started playing a game together. It was easy making friends when we were little, because there were no pressures or expectations. Not like now.

After the bus pulls into the school car park I walk into the (rank) hallway and see Whisper straight away. What are the goddamn odds? She's standing with a big group of boys from the year above. I recognise most of them, one is Captain of the rugby team. Dom, his name is. Dom the Dick, is what I think. I feel a bit nervous about approaching her when all these popular and sporty guys are around, so I perch down on the steps nearby and get my phone out to pretend to read. I'm not reading, obviously, I'm eavesdropping.

I watch as one of the boys puts his hand on her lower back. Ed, I think he's called.

"There's a party this Friday night at Wardy's. Free house. You should come," he tells her with a leer.

"Sounds good," she replies nonchalantly, as though she gets party invites all the time. She probably does.

"Yeah it's gonna be. Everyone's gonna be there. Everyone cool anyway, no weirdos."

"Who's weird?" she asks.

"That kid Nelson over there, for a start," he says. I bring my head lower and pray they can't see me going red. My skin burns and my fingers tighten around my phone as I feel them all turn to look at me.

"He seems cool to me," Whisper replies quietly. My heart is beating out of my chest. She thinks I'm cool? She's defending me? Why would she do that?

"Yeah, yeah. He's cool. I just meant he's a smart alec," Ed backtracks quickly.

"Well, that's not what you said," Whisper fires back at him. I daren't look up. My eyes are glued to the screen, staring at Max on my screensaver.

"How are you finding it here, anyway?" Dom asks, pushing in front of Ed slightly and saving him from Whisper's interrogation. He steps in front of Ed, his foot catching Ed's sneaker. Classic dominant male behaviour, swinging his metaphorical dick around to show him who's boss. Ed complies with the laws of nature and takes a step back, removing his hand from the small of Whispers back.

"Yeah, it's okay," she shrugs. "A bit boring."

"We could change that," a boy heckles from the back. They all chuckle and the corners of her mouth lift in a small smile. I can't tell if she thinks they're actually funny or not. I don't understand how anyone could find them remotely amusing, they're like a pack of desperate hyenas.

"Is this party really going to be all that then?" she asks, turning back to Dom.

"Yeah, everyone's coming," Dom tells her.

I roll my eyes. Obviously not *everyone*.

"My older brother's getting us loads of booze," Ed adds when she doesn't react.

"Save me a beer or two?" she asks Dom with a smile, ignoring Ed and reaching out to touch Dom's his arm tactically. She wants the free booze.

He responds as I knew he would, lapping up the attention. "Yeah, I could pull some strings and save you a couple of drinks. Keep it between us, yeah?" he tells her.

"It's my booze," Ed grumbles under his breath.

She makes a joke I don't hear and they all laugh.

I instantly feel jealous. Those big, beefy bastards. Alliteration has never felt so good to use. (Even better than Barfy Ben.) She's been at this school for two minutes and already has more people who know her name than people who would be able to pick me out of a goddamn line-up. How do some people have it so *easy*? Doesn't she worry what people think?

"Anyway, we've got to go to practice. Boys?" Dom rounds them all up with a wave of his hand and his baboons fall into line, Ed swinging a sack of rugby balls over his shoulder.

It feels like forever before they finally leave, Whisper turning back to her locker and inspecting her timetable, which she's pinned onto the door with flowery tape. I instantly get up and shuffle over to her.

Be confident. Be cool. Be anything other than Cooper-esque.

"So, where are you from?" I ask, leaning awkwardly against her locker. (Question one on my list, motivated by Mum's Question Time this morning.)

"Holy shit, where did you come from?" she looks around as though I've apparated out of thin air. One of my many traits is that people don't seem to notice I exist until I actually speak. It's a talent that until today, I've thanked God for. I mean, Ed literally pointed me out two minutes ago. I was right there.

"You ask a lot of questions, don't you? First pets, now past residencies…" she peers at me curiously, so close I can smell her flowery citrus perfume.

I say nothing and give a small shrug. Is asking a lot of questions bad? How do I start a conversation if I don't ask a lot of questions? It's not like I want to talk about myself.

"My family have just moved here from London," she replies after a pause. I let out a mental sigh of relief - she's still up for a conversation. "They thought it would be better for me to be in a smaller suburb, you know? Trying to straighten me out." She chuckles and tucks her hair behind an ear. It falls back to the front of her face. I fight the urge to push it back for her.

"I don't know what you mean by 'straighten out.' But I think it's pretty exciting to be from London, though I've never been," I admit.

"You've *never* been?" Her eyes widen slightly.

She's turning the conversational situation I had planned around, which makes me slightly nervous. I was prepared to ask her questions about herself, not answer ones about me. My hands clench and unclench automatically.

"Nope. Seems kind of busy," I mumble.

"Yeah, it is super busy. You're not missing out on much, it's a bit of a shithole really. Better than here though, there's sod all to do around here! You don't even have a 24 hour takeaway place. It's what my parents wanted though, I think they just want me to live a quieter life, go out less and focus on school and stuff. I'm not too keen on school though; I can't concentrate on things for too long," she continues, her plump lips moving quickly as she speaks.

I'm all ears.

She carries on, getting more excited by the second. "Hey, you're clever, aren't you? Maybe you can help me with some of my math homework sometime? This guy earlier saw you when you were texting and was saying you were a real brainbox." I mentally congratulate her on twisting what Ed said about me so positively.

"Anyways, I'm failing math at the moment and my Old Lady will go mental at me if I don't get a C and I can't be dealing with that agg,"

She talks and talks, and I listen and listen. How can she get so many words out in one breath? I'm flattered she would ask me for help and try not to cringe at her use of the word 'agg.'

"Of course, I'm happy to help you with your math," I say, even though it's really not my best subject. Words I can do, numbers - not so much. But as long as I'm better than she is, I'll be able to impress her and maybe get some one-on-one time with her to chat more. If she's struggling to get a

C, it should be okay as I'm on a C+. It should be fine. I hope it's fine. Please be fine.

"Amazing, thank you so much. I'll speak to you about it later, but I just have to run and meet this girl, Ellie, before next class," she explains and jogs away, shouting, "talk later?" over her shoulder at me as she joins another girl who has even more piercings than her.

She has been here one day and already has to meet someone before class. I've been here years and nobody has ever met me before anything. Except Suzie, who definitely does not count.

I stay in the spot because I'm not sure where to go before class starts. It's not like I have someone to meet, as we have already established. In the end I pull my phone out and text Prince.

- I spoke to The Girl.
Moments later my phone buzzes.

- Congratulations. Your text was read out to my entire class. No texting during school hours. Your friend has now had his phone confiscated until end of the day, when you may or may not hear back from him.

I stare down at my phone and finally shake my head and laugh. Goddamn PTS.

That night Prince texts me.

- You got my phone confiscated for the entire day man! But dw, I'll forgive you, I'm a great guy like that. What happened with The Girl?

- She wants me to help her with math, I text back.

- But you're shit at math?

- I know that, and you know that, but she doesn't know that, I reply.

- MY MAN! But how are you gonna pull this off?

- I just need to be good enough that I'm better than her. I think I already am, she's on a D.

- Shouldn't be a problem then, you suave fox.

I grin and put my phone down. But then my cycling thoughts start and I start to worry. Does she only want to hang out with me so I help her with her math? And then she'll go to the party at the weekend and drink alcohol with rugby guys and probably laugh about me behind my back... My hand curls into itself. What if she's better than she's making out? What if she's actually as good as me, and I turn up to help her and don't know the answers?

I rub the back of my neck, suddenly wide awake and full of dread. What have I gotten myself into?

I fall asleep that night with a math book on my face.

The next day I'm eating my lunch alone (as usual), when the chair beside me pulls out and it's Whisper. I blink at her a few times like she's going to disappear, and she says nothing but pulls out a notebook. I quickly brush my anxiety tablets into my backpack and pray she hasn't clocked them. I take them with food and if anyone asks I just say they're antibiotics. She doesn't seem to have noticed.

As she puts the notebook down beside me, I notice she has bruises on the very bottom of her wrists where they meet her palms. She must have tripped and used her hands to stop the fall - it's happened to me before and I was bruised in the exact same place.

"You fell?" I ask her.

She looks at me quizzically.

I glance down at her wrists.

"Oh, right," she says, pulling her sleeves down slightly. "Yeah, tripped going home yesterday."

"It's happened to me before, too," I tell her sympathetically. "Had bruises in the same place."

"Yeah, annoying." She smiles at me. "So, anyway, I need you to help me with the math I mentioned yesterday? See, I have this test next week and if I fail, I'm gonna be in trouble," she grumbles, pulling out a pencil case and her math textbook. "Maybe if you just run over it really, really quickly I might understand? Please?" She blinks her big blue eyes and long lashes at me, and I nod, my mouth dry.

Please be something I can do, please be something I can do, please be something I can do...

"It's on multiplying... binomials?" she says it as though she isn't sure she has the word correct.

I blink.

Fuck.

Then she flips through her book and finds the page and my entire body sags, I breathe out and grin. I know this! The only math thing in the whole goddamn world that I know. I pray to Gods I don't believe in and thank them.

"Timesing brackets," I tell her. "Do you know the smiley face method?"

She frowns at me. "Smiley face?"

"Yeah, it's really easy. So look," I pull her notebook over and she passes me her pencil. "You connect these and these... and then down here, and here, and look! It's a smiley face," I jab a finger at the paper triumphantly where I have transformed two bracket sums into a smiling face.

"Holy shit, it is a smiley face," she giggles.

"And then you can work it out from that," I say, explaining which bits connect and what to do with them as she nods along beside me. I'm so excited to have gotten something right that I almost don't notice the way that her face gets really intense when she's concentrating, or how she's wearing pink lipstick instead of red today and it somehow makes her complexion look like porcelain.

"It doesn't even feel like math when you do it this way," she says excitedly after completing her third exercise correctly.

"I know. It's like art," I grin back. I feel a frisson between us as we smile at each other and then it's broken when she hunches back down over her book scribbling away and drawing the smiley face over all her brackets.

"I'm gonna nail this test now. Thank you so much," she says, and then she leans over and hugs me. I'm so startled I don't respond for a moment, but then I wrap my arms around her. She is so small, so tiny and so fragile in my long, lanky grip. She's warm as well, it's like squeezing a little hot water bottle. I try and can't remember the last time I hugged someone properly like this, family doesn't count. And back-claps from Prince definitely don't count.

I'm a bit disappointed when she lets go.

I'm more disappointed when I don't see her again for the rest of the week.

***

Weekend's are generally spent drawing, reading, walking Max and hanging out with Prince. It's Saturday and I've woken up really early - I haven't been sleeping well recently. I feel restless all the time, but for once it's a nice kind of restless. Like I'm looking forward to living instead of hating it quite so much.

I decide to take Max for a pre-breakfast walk through the woods behind my house.

He looks like he's smiling as he trots next to me, his oversized ears flapping around on the floor. I love how he occasionally runs on ahead before stopping to check that I'm still following, as though he's telling me not to worry because he'll always wait for me to catch up.

There's a breeze and the leaves shake with the wind, but the sun is shining, and the twigs are crunching beneath my boots. It's very calming being in the woods. There's never anyone around except other dog-walkers who nod and say good morning and you get time to just be alone. To be utterly yourself, with nobody around to impress or to judge you. I watch as Max sniffs around in some moss and think about the math lunch with Whisper. I was lucky and I know it - if she had asked about any other topic I wouldn't have been so able to help. I hope she doesn't ask me for help again, but I also kind of hope she does. I wonder where she's been all week. After that lunch she was out of school, absent from class and no sign of her anywhere in the hallways. She must have gotten sick, but she seemed so fine at lunch it's weird that she got so sick so quickly. I hope she's ok.

When I get in, I decide to recreate Max in a drawing. I design him on two legs like a human and he's walking through the woods with his eyes shut, smiling. I add in a cape for good measure. Pretty much all of my caricatures have capes, superhero-inspired drawings are my nerdy weakness.

I'm just putting together the finishing touches on his collar when the door opens. "Cup of tea, dear?"

"I'm good thanks, Mum."

"What is it you're doing there, then?" she steps over and peers over my shoulder. "Oh, my! Is that Max?"

I nod.

"Well, Cooper, this is brilliant! My favourite you've ever done," she gushes. (She says this literally every time.) "This is to go straight on the fridge when you're finished," she adds, which makes me feel about six years old but still kind of proud.

Whenever a new drawing goes up on the fridge, the old one goes into a box of all my art I've done since I was a kid that she keeps. I sometimes look through the box at how much I've improved to inspire me to keep on going. I get ideas for my college portfolio from it too.

I've never shown anyone the box. Not even Prince. He thinks sketching is kind of lame, although he doesn't make fun of me for liking it. He thinks anything that doesn't involve a remote control or boobs is lame. I sometimes wonder why he hangs out with me so much.

I'm about to go back to my drawing when I notice that Mum hasn't left. She's sat herself down on my bed awkwardly and is looking at me.

"You waiting for a bus?" I ask her.

"No. Well, it's just that I thought we could have a chat. You haven't mentioned your new friend again, I was wondering how that was all going," she says gently.

Jesus, my mother feels sorry for me. She's checking up because she knows Prince is my only friend. I'm pathetic. "Fine," I tell her.

I expect her to stand up to leave, but she doesn't, she just carries on sitting there and waiting for me to continue.

I sigh, as though very tired. "She hasn't actually been in all week," I admit.

"Oh dear. Is she unwell?" Mum asks.

I shrug. "I don't know, I just haven't seen her around," I mumble. I can't stop wondering why I haven't seen her around. Where is she? I wring my hands together and pick up my pencil to stop myself.

"New environment, poor pet probably is struggling to settle in," Mum says, nodding to herself.

"Yeah, probably just struggling to settle in," I repeat quietly, chewing on the end of my pencil as Mum sees herself out of my bedroom.

CHAPTER 3

BIG MOUTHS

On Monday I spot her in the hall, the same spot where I saw her last time with the rugby boys, near the girl's toilets and leaning against her locker, tapping away on her phone. Gangly legs, ebony hair scraped half-up. She's wearing tights and a giant hoodie that swamps her frame, little black leather boots grounding it all.

"Where have you been?" I ask as I approach her. I've wondered all week, and it fell out of my mouth before I could think of a more charming way of greeting her.

"Busy," she replies.

"Too busy for school?"

"I'm always too busy for school," she says with a grin. It's clear she doesn't want to tell me where she's been or why she was off, and I don't want to pry. Maybe she's been really sick. Maybe it's 'girl stuff.' Bella takes time off sometimes because of cramps and she stays at home groaning and watching sad films on purpose to make herself cry. I want to speak with Whisper about something normal - definitely *not* cramps - and remember the party she was invited to by the rugby boys. I'm pretty sure it's the same party I overheard some kids discussing on the bus this morning - apparently someone kicked a hole in a garden shed or something. It's an obvious topic of conversation which might even make it seem like I'm 'in the know' of the social calendar, but like I had somewhere even cooler to be. I give myself a mental pat on the back for being so wily.

"So, how was the party at the weekend?"

"Very fucking funny. So you know too. Well done you, pat on the back. Fuck off, pervert!" she snaps at me, red faced and wild-eyed. She swings her bag onto her back aggressively, slams her locker and storms off, her leather boots stomping on the squeaky floor.

I flinch at the echoing sound of the metal locker door slamming and clench and unclench my fists, my chest rising and falling quicker as I feel myself get hot and red. People heard, they're all turning and looking at me. They think I've done something wrong. They're staring at me. They're laughing at me. They're noticing me. Clench. Unclench. They know I've done something bad to upset her. But did I? Maybe I have, I'm so confused, but right now I just need to *get out of here.*

I stumble into the men's bathroom where I sit in a stall with my head in my hands and try to steady my panicked breathing. Clench, unclench. So many people were looking at me. My fringe is sticking to my forehead, sweat slick. Why did she have to shout at me? Everyone goddamn heard. They all think I'm a pervert. They all think I'm a pervert. They all think I'm a pervert. Pervert, *pervert*, goddamn pervert. I want to text Prince, but he might get in trouble again. I need to speak to someone. I need advice. I need to calm down. I need to fix this. I need to run.

43

I've never fallen out with anybody before, definitely not a girl. What are people going to be saying about me?
I need to speak to someone. Right now.
I rush through the corridors keeping my head down. Every sound I hear I'm convinced it's people speaking about me. I'm outside Suzie's office, my knee jiggling uncontrollably, hands wringing, fingers aching. I can't stop fidgeting and don't try to stop my knee bouncing because if I do my head will spin and I'll barf. I look down at the carpet and focus on a questionable-looking yellow stain and I breathe and I breathe and I breathe.

After what feels like ten thousand years, Suzie opens her door and lets a girl who looks like she's been crying out of her office. Before she's even finished her 'come back if you need to talk again' spiel, I've stormed into the room like a rhino in heat, slamming the door behind me.

I start trying to explain but she does a downwards motion with her hands and tells me I'm speaking too quickly. "Deep breaths Cooper, and slow down. From the beginning again. S-l-o-w-l-y," she says gently, taking a seat behind her desk.

I know she wants me to sit down but I can't, so I pace around the room which is so small I only make it three strides before having to turn around and I start getting dizzy. Why is the goddamn room so small?

"I asked this girl how her weekend was and she called me.. She called me a goddamn pervert and everyone was looking at me and I think everyone heard and they'll all be talking about it-" I ramble on and on and I go over the conversation word by word and the more I speak about it the dryer my mouth gets until I can taste imaginary vomit on my tongue.

Suzie can obviously read my mind because she goes to the water cooler and puts a glass of water in front of me wordlessly.

"Look, Cooper. Calm down. Clearly there has been a misunderstanding. It sounds like this girl thought you were insinuating something or making fun of something that you actually don't know about. It's all a big mistake so you just need to apologise and explain that you don't know what she was referring to," Suzie tells me after I've finished.

"But what about all the other people? Everyone heard and laughed and that might stick with me for the rest of my life," I breathe the words out quickly.

"What might stick with you, Cooper?" Suzie asks gently.

"The word 'pervert,'" I whisper, looking at the floor.

"But you aren't, Cooper. You know you aren't, and all you can do is be true to yourself. If people try to upset you or wind you up, they're just looking for a reaction and you should ignore them. Hold your head high because they are wrong. Know yourself and believe in yourself." She leans forward, her hands in her lap.

"I shouldn't say this, but you must remember this is just highschool. Some bit of juicy gossip will happen at lunchtime and everyone will forget about your interaction this morning. A small outburst between two people won't be a big deal in the long run, even though I know it feels like it right now."

She sits back in her chair and watches me carefully. I feel slightly better, knowing that logically, she is correct. But physically my heart rate is still up, my skin is still sweating and I still have to fight the urge to glance around the room every two seconds in search of a threat. Clench, unclench.

Suzie has to be right, this is an easy misunderstanding to resolve. I just need to explain myself. And make sure everybody knows that I am, categorically, not a pervert. I breathe in and out slowly, counting to ten in my head before I realise that Suzie is counting along in the background with me. My palms ache so I unclench my hands slowly, fingers twitching with the desire to curl up again and dig the nails into my skin. Eventually, my sweat cools and dries, my mouth feels damp again and my head doesn't feel dizzy and crowded. I sigh and stand up slowly.

"And Cooper?"

I turn to face Suzie, my hot hand on the doorknob.

"Are you sure you can't tell me who the girl is? She may need some help?"

I shake my head. "I can't. Snitches…"

"Get stitches. I know, I know." She gives me a sad smile and waves me out.

There are two kids already waiting to see her outside the office.

I go to my science class but when Whisper's name is called out for the register, it goes unanswered. I glance around the room. She's not here. Again. Where is she? Why does she always disappear like this? Is it because of me?

I lean over to the girl next to me, Bryony, to ask if she knows. Everyone calls her Boring Bryony because she has no opinions on anything. I translate this into the idea that she only ever speaks the truth. I don't think this makes her boring, I like it. I like it because I know she's never said bad things about me, and I know she never makes fun of me. She just says it how it is.

Boring Bryony leans back and tells me, "Whisper's bunking for a smoke."

I nod, as though this is what I had expected all along, and Bryony goes back to chewing her pen lid, gnawing at it like a guinea pig.

I've never bunked class. Not that many people do, to be honest. You can get suspended if you're caught, and also if you're smoking. I wonder if Whisper could get suspended twice for doing both at once, but I'm pretty sure it doesn't work that way. Maybe she even *wants* to get suspended. She doesn't seem to like it here, and I'm pretty sure if she's bunking today she was probably skipping school last week, too. She must hate it.

I've never smoked either. I hate the smell, it seems to cling to my curtains from Prince's visits and always makes me feel a little queasy in the mornings. I don't think I've ever actually told him how much I hate it. Thing is, he's my best friend, and sometimes you put up with the little annoyances because it's worth it. I like that he comes round all the time, and I can't imagine him coming round and not smoking. It's just part of who he is, ever since we were 13 and he started secretly smoking at PT school. I couldn't believe it at the time - I was such a goody-goody kid. But for him it wasn't a big deal, just like I bet bunking isn't a big deal for Whisper.

I wonder why she decided to bunk class by herself. Most people do it with friends so they can hang out together, but to skip class by yourself seems kind of a lonely, sad thing to do. Especially when it's clear that she already has more people wanting to hang out with her from this school than I have in my whole life.

47

I'm pretty sure Prince has skipped school as well, snuck back home when his parents are at work to play video games. Which is also pretty sad, to be honest.

I need to keep my brain occupied so I don't stress about what I'll say to Whisper when I see her, and also how I'll clear my name, so I spend the rest of the class making a definitive list of the things I would do if my mum worked and I could get away with bunking off school to sneak back home.

I write it in the back of my workbook. My knee shifts up and down like it's vibrating for most of the lesson, but there's nothing I can do about that.

Cooper's list for bunking:
1. Watch porn on the big tv instead of on my phone, hiding under the covers.
2. Make a giant sandwich with all the dumb-ass things I want in it, like crisps and cheese strings.
3. Go through Bella's room and search for future blackmail material.
4. Buy all the pizza I want and eat it all in front of the tv watching fantasy films.
5. Walk around butt-naked.

When I'm done, I rip it out and scrunch it into a ball, pushing it to the bottom of my bag. I'll stick it in my private art journal at home, it'll make me laugh one day.

As the class comes to an end and everybody begins filtering out, discussions about the party at the weekend begin to take over the conversation.

"His parents came home early and he hadn't told them about the party. His dad went mental!" A girl is whispering conspiratorially.

"Oh my God, then what happened?"

"Well, they threw everyone else out, obviously! I just ran, in case they called the police or something. Apparently he's not allowed anywhere other than his house and school for three whole months."

"My parents would ground me for an entire year if I threw a secret party," the other girl replies with disbelieving eyes.

I wonder what my mum would do if she came home and found I had decided to throw a house party. She would probably keel over in shock that I had anybody to invite, for a start. Then double over again at the fact that anyone I had invited had actually turned up. I imagine that having a house party would lead to awkward social interactions and definitely at least one stressful barfathon, so I won't be attending one any time soon, let alone hosting one.

"It wasn't even that big, there was only kids from our year there. It wasn't a rager or anything," the girl continues, her voice tinged with sympathy for the boy.

Then this girl, Laura, turns around from her locker to join in the conversation. Her hips are stuck out to one side, and her hair is pulled up into a tight side ponytail, making her facial features look tight and strained. She never has anything nice to say about anyone. Everyone says she's the Bitch of the School and as far as I'm aware, nobody ever stands up to her because it's not ever worth incurring her wrath.

Whenever she walks near me, I shrink into myself, hoping she won't notice me and say something catty that everybody else will hear.

I like to tune out when people like Laura are around, I tend to feel as though just listening to their opinions and stories will make me instantly less intelligent. Stupidity is often contagious. My Dad once said, people with big mouths and small brains are the worst kind of person. I think he was talking about Trump when he said it, but I assume it can apply to anyone.

"It wasn't even that great a party, there was barely any gossip," Laura says with an eyebrow raised.

The two girls shrug, almost as though apologising to Laura.

"Oh," she adds with a smirk. "Other than what happened with that new girl, Whisper. What a dirty whore! No wonder she's not here today, I'd be too ashamed to show my filthy face for weeks. Imagine giving a blowie to a guy so soon after starting a new school. I heard she's riddled with STDs. Easier than feeding a starving dog." She starts to cackle with laughter and people around her nervously join in. "Seriously, who does she think she is? Flouncing in here thinking she's a big deal from London. She's nobody here and she was probably nobody back in London too. You know, I heard she got expelled from her last school for being caught having sex in the school toilets. Can you imagine? Disgusting slut should learn to keep her legs closed or -" and I never found out what the 'or' would have been, because I lunge at Laura.

Now I've lunged, I don't really know what to do because my parents always taught me you must never hit a woman. All I know is I feel an all-consuming rage of injustice for

Whisper swarm over me like a storm of locusts. I'm just so angry at the unfairness of it all, of speaking so badly about someone in front of so many people.

I push Laura, knocking her to the ground. She's screaming at me and clawing at my face with her ratchet fake nails and I just hold her down there because I can't bloody hit her. Someone lifts me off her and punches me on her behalf.

I stagger backwards. I don't know who it was that hit me, but I can taste warm copper as my mouth fills with blood. People have gathered around Laura protectively and a few people are stood beside me as though waiting to pull me away from her again. I hear someone call me a psycho. She's wailing and clutching her hand and two of her fake nails are lying forlornly beside her, like residue of a vicious fight. It almost makes me want to laugh.

I look at her and tell her, "People with big mouths and small brains are the worst type of person, Laura."

I spit blood on the floor and a bit of it flies from my lips and onto her face, which is pale and shell-shocked.

The place is horribly silent for a really long time until Mrs Hayward pushes through the crowds and grabs me.

"Cooper Nelson! Mr Gray's office, NOW!"

That's when I realise that for the first time in a long time, I'm not anxious.

I'm angry.

Scarily, it feels good. It feels good to have my head focused on only one thing, on how angry I am at Laura and how cruel she is. I feel brave and like I don't care what anyone thinks of me because I know I was doing the right thing. Like Suzie said, I *know* myself. I know what I stand for, and I know when sticking up for someone else is more important than being afraid. I let the feelings of anger run through me as I close my eyes and breath, the relief of not feeling so goddamn afraid all the time washing over me in a nice warmth. I am okay. I am okay. I am okay.

I'm sat outside Mr Gray's office waiting. My knee is still. My hands rest in my lap. It wasn't right, what Laura was saying. You can't talk about people like that, and she was doing it loudly on purpose. She wanted people to hear, she wanted to humiliate someone who wasn't there to defend herself. It was wrong. And what does she know, anyway? She could have been lying, or making it up for attention. I don't know if Whisper would do those things. I don't care even if she did, it was still wrong to call her out in the hallway like that, to taint everyone's opinions of her when she's new.

The door to the reception bursts open and Jesus Christ, it's my goddamn parents.

"Cooper, your parents have arrived," the receptionist informs me, as though I am suddenly blind. "You may now go into Mr Gray's office."

"Cooper? Is everything okay?" Mum is instantly at my side, grabbing at me as though checking for broken bones. "What happened to your face?"

I shrug her off me and say nothing. My Dad looks very stern and serious as we step into Mr Gray's office and we all sit down in front of his desk. It's as though my parents are being told off alongside me. Told off for having such a disruptive and explosive son.

I stare resolutely at the floor.

Mr Gray sighs a long, slow breath as though he is very tired, and he rubs his temples.

"Mr and Mrs Nelson, unfortunately we're here today because your son got into an altercation this afternoon between classes."

"Altercation?" my dad asks, his brows furrowed.

"Yes. According to various witnesses he assaulted Laura Stokeman."

"Assaulted?" my mother wails.

I cringe, but stay silent.

"Yes. And due to the amount of hullabaloo that the interaction caused, I fear I have no choice but to suspend Cooper."

My mother makes a small gasping sound, as though she is being choked. Dad groans.

"He will have to leave with you today and will not be welcomed back onto the premises until Monday morning. I have a letter here to clarify everything and I'm sure you both appreciate, I don't want to be having this conversation again. Next time I won't be able to be so lenient."

He looks at me pointedly and I bow my head.

"That's all." He adds, effectively dismissing us.

My father stands and shakes his hand, my mum is looking at the floor as though she is a guilty convict. We shuffle out in silence and remain in silence all the way through the empty corridors until we get into the car.

"What the hell happened?" Dad finally erupts as soon as the car doors shut.

"It wasn't like he said. I didn't *assault* anybody. I... I pushed her." I admit, my voice quiet. I'm ashamed of myself. I know it was wrong to have lashed out like that, I don't know what came over me.

53

"You pushed a *girl*?" Mum asks, running a hand through her hair and shaking her head.

"She clawed me! And I got punched," I point out, pointing to the newly-formed bruise appearing on the side of my face.

Mum turns around and inspects my war wounds with concern, before deciding that I will go on to live a long and healthy life and contorting her face back into her disappointed frown.

"But why?" she asks again, turning back to face the road.

"She was being horrible about someone, I was sticking up for them."

In the rear-view mirror I see my mother's face soften and she glances at my dad.

He says nothing for a moment, and then, "I got pulled out of bloody work for this."

When we arrive home, I go to head up to my room.

"It really wasn't how Mr Gray made out-" I start to say when I'm halfway up the stairs, my parents' disappointment coursing through the back of my head like an electric shock.

"Cooper, tonight is not the night to hear your reasoning. Tonight is the night to be angry. Tomorrow you can reason, but you are grounded for the week," my mum tells me.

I nod and go up to bed. Seems fair enough.

I text Prince to keep him updated on the situation and to let him know he'll have to go elsewhere if he wants to smoke this week.

His response is helpful as always.

- DUDE, YOU BEAT UP A GIRL?! That's fucked up!
Followed by many laughing face emojis.

I lie back in bed and stare at the ceiling, thinking about the events of the day.

The things Laura said that Whisper had done - I don't believe them. I don't know if I can't believe it, or if I don't want to believe it. I think the line is thin between the two. But one thing is for sure - I've decided that even if she has done those things Laura said she did, it doesn't make her a bad person. And I don't regret sticking up for her when she wasn't there to stick up for herself. Now I understand why she was angry at me this morning. I've been interacting with someone at my school for less than a week and I've already screwed it up, somehow. Me and my goddamn stupid questions.

CHAPTER 4

TRUANT

The next morning I wake up with a mixture of happiness that I get the day off school, and shame for the day before. I got called a pervert and pushed a girl all within two hours. I am a disgraceful human being and barely slept as a result, going over my altercation with Laura in my head approximately five hundred times, each time imagining it from someone else's point of view and envisioning different reactions from myself that perhaps would have been more appropriate. My eyes are decorated with deep blue circles to match my bruise.

On the bright side, as a consequence for my actions I have effectively been gifted a week to lie-in for as long as I want and draw as much as I want. I try to remind myself of what Suzie said, but this wasn't just passing comments in the hallway. It was a full-on physical fight. Between myself and a girl. It's going to take more than a week for this to blow over, but I'm glad I'm away from everyone while it's all so fresh. Of course, I'd never let my parents know these feelings and am sure to paint the picture of guilt onto my face as I come downstairs with my proverbial tail between my legs. Mum purses her lips at me, but pours me a cup of coffee nonetheless.

I'm just spreading Marmite on my toast when my phone lights up with an unknown number flashing on the screen. Perhaps it's just a wrong number, or it could be a telemarketer… but then the phone rings again with the same number and my rational side is soon drowned out by the panic that grips me. Who is it? Why are they calling me? How did they get my number? Is it because of what happened yesterday? I freeze, butter-knife suspended in mid-air. My chest begins to seize up and tighten, panic flooding into my veins. My free hand clenches tightly. I'm always more anxious after no sleep.

The thought of answering a call without knowing who it is or what it's about makes me feel sick, so I leave it and watch it flash until it rings out. When it stops buzzing on the table I let out a sigh of relief and resume spreading Marmite. My mother eyes me suspiciously.

"Telemarketer," I lie as explanation. "Keep calling about an accident I may or may not have been involved in."

She nods and walks out without comment, The Morning Show switching on in the background.

A few moments later as I sit eating my toast at the table, my phone screen lights up again, only this time it's a message.

I peer at the screen and see it's the unknown number again, but I can read the short message preview.

- **Yo! It's Whisper.**

My stomach flips when I read that, but in the good way, not the barfathon way. Then I remember she thinks I'm a pervert and it flips in the barfathon way.

- I hope you don't mind me tracking down your number - it was pretty hard to do. Bit of a lone wolf aren't you? I'm messaging you for 2 reasons.

1st--I heard what happened between you and Laura and I think what you did was super nice and brave. Nobody has ever stood up for me like that before. It was so cool what you did and I really appreciate it. I don't know why you did it, but I'm grateful. Thanks.
2nd-- I'm sorry for how I spoke to you that other morning, I thought you were making a dig at me. You're not a perv, I'm just a psycho
3rd -- Maybe when you're back we can hang out or something?
(Told you I was bad at math.)
W x

I think for ages about how to reply. So long that my toast goes cold. I have to play this cool, I can't mess it up now. The beauty of texting is I can come across as much more confident because I have a chance to think about what I'm saying and analyse how it might be taken by the recipient.
I chew my lip, I sweat a little (okay, a lot) and eventually I end up with this:

- Hey Whisper. That's okay, sorry if I hurt your feelings anyway. I did what I did, partly because Laura is a bitch and should never have said those things about you, but partly because I'd like to be your friend. I'd like to hang

with you when I'm back on Monday. I got called a psycho, so we can be psychos together. See you then, Cooper x

My thought process behind the message was that it was important to apologise for upsetting her even though it was an accident and also that I didn't want her to think I only pushed Laura because I was defending her honour, because that might be creepy.

She doesn't reply. I keep waiting for one, but it doesn't come. I go over my message about fifty times and tell myself that I didn't really leave her an entry to reply, that my message unintentionally ended the conversation. It's always my fault when things don't go as hoped.

***

The week drags on slowly, but I plough through it. I spend an embarrassing amount of hours wondering why Whisper didn't reply to my text, if I said the wrong thing, what I should have said instead, if I should text again (Prince says never double text). I don't sleep very much, but eventually I decide I wouldn't have done it differently and now I just have to live with the consequences. Usually I can't come to conclusions like this so easily, but I feel safer and calmer at home, like I can be myself and nobody is judging me or talking about me. I try to sketch but they all come out distorted and not how I envision them. Not cool distorted, like Picasso. Crappy distorted. I get so frustrated I end up giving up and reading instead. I even watch a couple of animal documentaries with my parents, because hell, who else am I going to speak to?

By Sunday night I'm so nervous about going back to school that I'm jittery all day, my knee jumping and my fingers twitching. At night I can't sleep and just lay there, restless and awake as I think about all the potential ways this new friendship could go and wondering if people are still talking about the fight. My anxiety sets in and contorts all my excitement about seeing Whisper into fear and all the great things about friendship twist their way into becoming all the terrible things about friendship. We could argue again, she could be using me, she could realise she hates me, she could turn the whole school against me, she could think I'm a pervert after all…

When morning comes, I'm a nervous wreck. I make it into school somehow, the journey a long and sweaty blur. I hope I can pull myself together. I end up going to the bathroom to try to dry my shirt out a little under the hand dryer. I realise how pathetic this is, but at this point I don't really care. I am one moist mess.

I need to pull myself together in case I see Whisper. I can just imagine myself doing something embarrassing like opening my mouth to speak and dribbling all over myself. (This happened to me once in year eight when the teacher asked me a question, I had been just about to fall asleep. I was so embarrassed I tried to convince my mum to sign me up for homeschooling.)

"Hey, weirdo." Whisper jumps on me in the hallway and catches me off guard, her hand grabbing my waist and swinging herself round to face me. I thank the heavens I don't let a fart slip out - it's been known to happen when I get startled. I also don't dribble on myself, so I consider the interaction a win so far.

"Hi," I say.

Please, please don't let my sweat patches be showing.

"So listen, I'm totally not up for going to math today. Want to skip with me?"

A red light shoots up. If I were to go along with this suggestion it would involve skipping a class. I have only just gotten back from suspension, and I'm not keen to get suspended again any time soon. My second thought is that surely if she wanted to get better at math, the last thing she should be doing is skipping it? But mostly what I pick up on is the fact that she had asked *me* to skip class with her. Which means she wants to spend time with me. This definitely meant I was categorized as a potential friend. My head starts battling it out; my rational, good-Cooper side versus my Whisper-ised, new-born-rebel side.

I find myself agreeing enthusiastically, as if I'm a regular truant.

"Great," she grins at me. "Meet me at the back of the school by the bench in fifteen minutes? I'm just going to go pick some stuff up."

"Sure."

I watch her skip off down the hall and immediately begin to regret my decision. I should not have agreed to skip class. If my parents find out I will be in indefinite trouble. Maybe I could just go to class? But then I'd be ditching her and she'd be waiting for me and the potential friendship would be over before it even started. Clench. Unclench.

No, I have a better idea. I'll skip math, and then afterwards I'll go speak to the teacher and explain I missed it because I had been throwing up. Then he'll probably tell me to go to the nurse and I'll say I've already been and that will be that. Damn, I'm good.

I sneak out as the bell goes and everyone around me is bustling to get to class. As usual, nobody notices me. By the time I get to the back of the building where the park bench is, Whisper is already there waiting for me. I'm nervous, but seeing her sitting there waiting for me makes me feel good.

"Hey! So, where do you want to go?" she asks, standing from the bench.

I have no clue where I want to go - I'm not the master of truancy here, she is! She is supposed to know where we are going, how we are getting there, and how we are doing it without getting caught. My chest begins to feel tight. My fingers clench into my palms.

"I don't know. Wherever you want to go, I guess," I choke out.

She shrugs, as though deciding which side dish to order at Nandos. "Okay. Well, we can just go to the grassy bit with the trees around the back of the park if you like? Nobody will see us there, we can sit under the bank bit."

"Sounds good." I feel my shoulders relax a little. She has this worked out. This will be okay. We will not get caught.

We set off through the park and I can smell her sweet, musky perfume when the breeze comes my way.

"So seriously, thanks for the other day. With Laura, I mean."

I don't look at her, but I can feel her looking at me. Her voice is sincere, and she's dropped her tone as though confiding in me. There's a slight awkward pause and I feel myself go red. Again. This constant transition my skin undergoes every time I'm in her presence is tiring and frustrating. "No worries, it's fine," I reply, trying to sound nonchalant, as though I defend damsels every day.

"What was she saying about me?"

This time I feel my neck burning as I go an even deeper red. I don't know if I should tell her. Suzie says you should never say something to people which might hurt their feelings, and pretty much everything Laura had said about Whisper was nasty.

"Nothing that bears repeating," I reply eventually, which is the truth.

"Bitch," mutters Whisper, jamming her hands into her puffer coat pockets.

We walk along in silence again for a short while, mostly because she's stewing and partly because I have no idea what topic of conversation to bring up after that. But it's not a horrible awkward silence, like when a teacher asks you a question and everyone else seems to know the answer except you. It's a nice silence, like when you're listening to a really good song on the radio with someone else and you are both just enjoying the music. It's a beautiful song.

"Tell me about yourself?" I ask eventually. It was a shame to break the golden silence, but there's so much about her that I want to know.

"Curiosity killed the cat!" she smiles at me, her eyes sparkling.

I swallow.

"I'm boring as hell. I want to know about you! Dark lone wolf, mysterious knight in shining armour… you're a mystery," she tells me, pushing some tree branches out of her way as she leads me down a path littered with leaves and cigarette butts. We aren't the first of Bennessons' student body to have ambled down this trail.

I focus on my response, desperate not to tarnish the version of myself that she has created in her mind. She seems to think I'm an enigma, when in fact she is the most intriguing person I have ever met. I'm not sure how to take this. I think I'm flattered.

"I like to draw," I tell her finally.

"Oh cool! What do you draw?"

She's interested in me, in my hobbies? This is a serious first, when it comes to girls. Or people in general, really. "Everything. People, places, animals…"

"Will you draw me?" she asks.

I smile self-consciously and nod. A sudden image flashes into my mind, a scene re-enacted from Titanic where Whisper is naked on a vintage lounger and I'm painting her into what will one day be a masterpiece worth millions. I cough self-consciously and stare resolutely at my sneakers, trying to erase the image from my head before I overheat and die.

"Amazing." She grins and throws her backpack onto a grassy bank below us.

She was right - there really is nobody around here to catch us skiving. It feels like our own private place. The grass is quite thin but there are trees surrounding us, their leaves orange from the cold, but there's still enough foliage to act as a canopy, like a giant umbrella hiding us away in our little dip in the ground. She unwraps her black scarf and lays it out on the ground like a blanket before sitting on it.

"Do you have any hobbies?" I ask, sitting down beside her. She's lounging back like she's on a sunbed, but I can't pull that off. I half-sit, half-lean beside her feeling awkward but too self-conscious to reposition myself.

"Nah. I used to like doing sporty stuff like netball, but I stopped. I don't know why. I don't really do anything…" she starts to rummage in her bag. "Gotcha!" she announces, producing a bright pink glittery lighter. It has a picture of a unicorn on it. I wonder where she got it from. It's ridiculous and over the top, just like she is.

"Got it online," she grins at me, as though she can read my mind. After a bit more rummaging she produces a small bag with little greeny bits in it that look like oregano.

"And now, the *piece de resistance!*" she declares, waving the bag in the air like a little flag of friendship. I know what the bag means - it means trouble.

"Want to split a spliff, babe?" she asks, although she's already started getting other bits out of her bag and expertly making one like a skilled artisan, her black nails moving quickly as her thin fingers grind and roll away.

I shake my head. "Er, no thanks."

"Oh. Really? Why not?" She stops rolling and looks up at me, disappointment on her face. Clench. Unclench.

I think back to all the lectures I've had from parents and teachers, the ads I've seen in magazines and on TV about drug abuse. When I think back to all these factors, my answer is simple. "Drugs kill." I'm only half-joking. I know cannabis rarely affects anyone life-threateningly, but knowing my luck I'd be one of the 1% who had one drag and go crazy for the rest of my life.

She throws her head back and erupts into the loudest and most contagious laughter I have ever heard. So much so that before long I find myself laughing too, until I'm clutching my sides with pain and tears stream down my face. We laugh together for what feels like years, until finally, through gasping breaths she says, "nobody ever died from weed."

"Well, they never put that in the ads, do they?" I reply curtly, grinning as she breaks into a new fit of laughter, brushing the tears from her eyes.

"That was a good one," she tells me as she continues rolling, her fingers working rapidly and precisely whilst I watch with fascination. So similar to Prince, but she's mixing it all up with the tobacco. When she's satisfied with her finished piece, she lights it and inhales deeply, letting out a big grin as she exhales. "See? It's easy. Try it."

She passes me the burning roll of paper. It doesn't smell quite as bad as a cigarette but I'm still unsure, the term gateway drug in the back of my mind. My mother would faint with horror if she saw me right now.

I don't want to do it, but I also don't want to not do it. I don't want her to think I'm seriously uncool and a pussy, on top of being socially awkward. Being socially awkward is unfortunately unavoidable for me, although I've played it pretty well so far.

And so I smoke it. I copy what she did, I take a deep breath in and damn, do I ever choke. I cough and splutter and she laughs and hoots at me. My throat is burning and my mouth tastes of shit.

With a strange sense of determination I try again, and this time I don't choke up. She counts down with me until I can

A Girl Called Whisper

blow it out and then I pass it back to her because that's more than enough experimenting for one day, if you ask me. I shake my head at her and wave my hands to signify the end of my adventurous behaviour.

She finishes the rest of the spliff by herself and I sit and wait for something weird and wonderful to happen to me, but nothing does. I just feel sleepy and heavy, as though ropes are tying me down to the grass where I'm sat.

We lay down beside each other on the scarf and stare up at the sky. We play a game where you make animals out of the clouds. I find some pretty good ones but she finds even better ones. Sometimes I can't see them, like when she swears she can see a rabbit with a top hat on, riding a camel. Damn, does she laugh when she finds that one. I can't see it though. Perhaps my imagination isn't as artistic as I thought.

"You know what, Cooper Nelson? You're alright," she tells me.

"I think you're pretty great, Whisper With No Last Name," I reply.

She laughs. "Are you chirpsing me?" she grins.

I don't know what chirpsing is so I don't reply. She does the mind-reading thing again and tells me, "that's London slang. It means flirting." Then she rolls her blue eyes like it was the most obvious thing in the world.

"I doubt it. I don't know how to flirt," I tell her, which is the truth.

"I'll teach you," she replies, and gets up.

I follow her and we walk quietly through the park for a bit. It's mostly mums and babies out. The sun is still out and it's starting to get quite mild so she rolls up her sleeves. When

—
67

she does, I see hundreds of little scars. Cuts, all up and down her arms. I know what they're from, I've read about it. I'm shocked but I can't seem to tear my eyes away from them. I've never seen so many. I know Suzie won't approve of me asking as it's too personal and may make her uncomfortable, but I can't stop myself. "Why do you cut yourself, Whisper?"

"These aren't cuts, they're war wounds," she grins at me, but this time her eyes are glazed over and don't smile alongside her mouth.

"Who is the war with?" I ask carefully.

"My stepdad," she replies. And that was that. I don't ask any more questions. Besides, I'm not prepared to come up with any advice if I heard the answers.

CHAPTER 5

POISON INK

"Can you be very sad and happy at the same time?" I ask my mum as I push food around my plate at dinner. I've been thinking about this question since seeing Whisper's arms.

The table goes quiet for a moment, a clatter of cutlery as my parents register my question and consider an answer. Bella munches noisily whilst watching the interaction with interest.

Finally, Mum tells me, "No, you are either very sad or very happy. You can't be both at once. Why do you ask, love?" I can see she has suspended chewing, and despite the fact she has put on an easy-breezy tone, she's worried.

"There's someone at school who always seems happy and they're always smiling and joking. But they do things that I think only really sad people do." I don't want to go into too much detail, it feels like a breach of trust.

Dad raises his eyebrows and Mum clears her throat awkwardly. "Well, Cooper, sometimes the saddest people of them all are the ones who hide it the best," she tells me.

I think about this for the rest of dinner, zoning in and out of the mundane family small talk. What's she hiding? Is the problem with her stepdad like when me and Bella argue over the TV remote, or is it deeper than that? It must be worse. Terrible, even. My hand drops to my pocket where my phone is, but I pull it back up to my fork. I don't want to be overbearing. Texting her may just seem nosy, overstepping the mark. It isn't my place to ask about family issues and she probably would have told me more if she'd wanted to talk to me about it. I sigh and stab a piece of chicken.

  After dinner I go upstairs and get out the angel painting inspired by Whisper that I made when I first met her. I add on plasters up and down her arms, each inked with tiny graphic-style stories of strength and hope. I even include a tiny unicorn on one, inspired by her lighter. If I can't fix her in real life, I can fix her in my painting. Then I slip it into a clear plastic envelope, so it doesn't get wrecked, and leave it by my bag to remember to take it in for her the next day. Gifts always cheer people up, so at least I can do my part without her explicitly knowing it's a cheer-up gift.

  I think about what Mum said as I go to sleep. Prince is the loudest person I know, he always seems happy - is he secretly sad? I don't think he is, and I know him as well as is possible. But perhaps nobody can ever know what someone else is truly thinking. People are so difficult to work out. And why don't I function the same way as everyone else? Why is it that when I panic I can't just hide it, cover it up and pretend it isn't happening? In fact, I can't really hide anything. I'm an open book. A portrait artist's dream. Why are we all so different?

The next morning I don't see Whisper until I get to history class for period two. She comes in a couple of minutes after me and comes straight for the seat next to mine, swinging her rucksack onto the desk.

"Morning, babe," she sings as she sits down, smiling.

I think about what Mum had said last night and now her smile doesn't seem quite as straightforward as it had before. If anything, it seems a little more beautiful and imperfect, as though it's hiding her secrets away for her. It makes me feel sad, like she's trying to be strong because she doesn't have anybody to be herself with.

"I brought something in for you today," I hiss to her. The teacher is already calling the register.

"Weird. I brought something in for you today, too," she replies, wiggling her eyebrows.

"Quiet during the register, please!" our teacher snaps.

Whisper rolls her eyes at me and sinks back into her seat, her mouth teased in a half-smile as though the teacher is the biggest imbecile she has ever met.

She brought me a gift? I wonder what it is. I wonder what it is for the entire period. I hope it isn't another spliff.

When the bell rings for break, we go outside to the concrete courtyard together and sit down on a bench. I pull out my illustration and give it to her. Please don't hate it, please don't laugh at me, why didn't I think this through earlier? This was the stupidest idea ever. *Please* don't hate it, please don't laugh at me...

"Oh my God!" she gasps. "Is this me?"

She looks happy, so I nod.

"I look so beautiful in this version," she says quietly, stroking the plasters on the painting. She smiles. "I love it.

Really, thank you, it must have taken ages." She leans over and gives me a hug. It's short but she's warm and her hair smells of flowery shampoo.

Then she turns around and pulls a book from her backpack, handing it to me.

"And this is for you. Since you said you liked art, I figured you would get more use out of it than me. It's a book all about Banksy, his history from Bristol and all his paintings. I think they're really cool, not that I know anything about art," she says to me as I flick through the pages.

"Thank you very much," I tell her. And I really mean it. Every year for Christmas, Prince gets me a new video game so he can come over and play it with me. Bella always gets me 'cool' clothes, my mum showers me with art material and my dad signs the card on Mum's gifts. But nobody has ever really given me anything so thoughtful before, just because. It makes me glow.

The bells ring again, and we're separated, me in art (obviously) with Whisper in music for our next class. Just before she leaves, I do something erratic. I wish I hadn't as soon as it's happened, but the words fall out of my mouth. "Would you like to come over for dinner next Friday?"

"So you can meet Max," I quickly add. She just looks at me with her brows furrowed.

"My dog," I clarify.

"Oh yeah, right. Sounds good, just text me when and where and I will be there," she tells me with a casual wave as she goes into her classroom.

I don't know why I did it, but it's done now, and I can't back out. What if she thinks my parents are painfully uncool and embarrassing and paints me with the same brush? Or she thinks our house is disgusting and lame? Are my parents going to interrogate her and make her uncomfortable? *Clench, unclench.*

I pull my phone out and text Prince.

- I invited a girl to my house for goddamn dinner!?!?!
He texts back a few moments later.

- Play it cool, my brother. A virgin you shall not remain.
I sigh and don't bother replying. My biggest worry right now is how to hold a conversation long enough to keep her entertained and make myself seem cool, not how to de-virginise myself in my parents' house while my mum is downstairs cooking chicken curry.

Sometimes I don't think Prince has any idea who I am. Or maybe he does and that's why he winds me up like this.

Eventually, I take my phone out of my pocket and text him again.

- Fuck off.

***

The rest of the week passes by strangely. Whisper became very quiet and closed off, not seeming to want to speak to me anymore. I wonder if it's because I invited her to dinner, but try to stay calm and remember the incident with the party mix-up. I must not blame myself unless it's clearly my fault. But what if it is my fault and I'm too stupid to realise it? Why has she suddenly stopped speaking to me?

It's the second day of being largely ignored, or grunted at, when I've sat down next to her and said hello. She pretends not to have heard me and continues scrolling through her phone before putting it back in her bag and staring blankly ahead at the whiteboard. *Clench. Unclench.* My chest feels a little tight, but I also feel annoyed. Why is it so hard for me to work out what's going on in everyone else's head? Why does she have to make it so *difficult*?

I sigh and remember this may not be about me. "Hey, is everything okay?"

"Fuck off and stop being nosey," she snaps, peering over her textbook.

I go red as I hear the two people sitting behind us giggle. Clench. Unclench. Swallow. My throat is goddamn dry. I bring my hands to my neck to hide the fact that I can feel my blush crawling its way down my neck and onto my chest, which is now prickly.

I leave Whisper alone. I'll get on with my life how I did before I met her and keep out of her way. I text Prince telling him she just snapped at me in front of everybody.

Prince texts back.

- She's probably on her period.

I don't know enough about girls to disagree. Instead, I tell myself that it wasn't my fault, I haven't done anything. I couldn't have done anything. Could I?

I stress about this for most of the day and when I get home I make a point of keeping myself busy by inviting Prince over to play video games.

"So you think she's gonna bail or something?" Prince asks, his tongue sticking out the side of his mouth as he tries to shoot at a masked raider.

"I dunno," I sigh. "We seemed cool, then she just snapped suddenly. Goddamn!" I throw my control down and Prince hollers as I get shot down by the opposition.

"Let's restart the game and make those bastards pay," he says solemnly, starting it all up again. "Well, girls love to cancel. If she hasn't cancelled, she's still coming. I wouldn't worry about that," Prince says diplomatically. "What I would worry about is how you're gonna hide what a geek you are from her." I can tell from his tone that he's messing with me, but I worry nonetheless as I look around my room.

Piles of videogames lie in one corner. My graphic novels line the bookshelves whilst my desk is a mass of papers, pens and sketches. Above my window are some old collectable figurines I still have from when I was young. Prince follows my eyeline. "Man, I was joking, but for serious? I'd hide those dolls."

"They aren't dolls, they're action figures," I grumble, but I know he's right.

"Just chill out. She's liked you enough to hang out so far. She can like you for who you are or she can get the hell out," he tells me, nudging me lightly.

"If she likes me for who I am, can I leave the figures out?"

"Nah, she's not ready for that yet," Prince grins. "Maybe hide them for now and take them out again once she's too in love with you to notice them."

I go red, but I can't help but smile.

We play until everything in my room looks mildly pixelated and when he leaves, I carefully place my figurines in a box under my bed.

Then the anxiety gets bad.

As soon as I lie down my head starts screaming.

It's YOUR fault Cooper, it's definitely your fault. You've upset her, you've humiliated her, you've disrespected her and now she doesn't want to be your friend anymore. Who can blame her? Nobody wants to be your friend. Prince only feels sorry for you, that's why he hangs out with you. Nobody likes you and you'll die alone. You think you'll fit in if you get to art school, but you won't. You'll be just as weird and alone as you are now, there's no logical reason to assume anything will change.

On and on and on it goes in my head. I can't stop it, I just lie there and listen to it clenching my fists until I get so exhausted that my eyeballs sting and after what feels like forever, I fall asleep.

On Thursday Whisper walks past me in the hallway, books in her arms. She nods at me but doesn't stop to chat. I notice she has a small bruise on one arm, a dark greyish blue against her pale skin, yellowing at one side. I wonder if she did it to herself or if somebody else did it to her, maybe her stepdad.

I don't ask. I'm a nosey fuck, just like she said I was.

I don't mention anything about the bruises and cuts to Suzie or Prince - it feels like I'm betraying Whisper by speaking about her problems and adopting them as my own. Instead I just worry and wonder about them. Wonder and wonder and wonder about Whisper, and if she's okay.

Then, out of the blue on Friday, just when I was beginning to accept that my new friendship was over before it ever really started, she bounces up to me when I'm at my locker.

"Hey, you!" She's grinning at me as though the past week of awkward interactions haven't existed, so much so that I find myself wondering if I imagined it all.

But even I'm not that crazy.

"Want to come into town with me after school?" she asks, popping a strawberry bubble of gum so that it deflates sadly, the faint smell of processed sugar puffing into my vicinity.

"Of course," I reply. If she's happy to pretend the last week hasn't happened, so am I, I tell myself. Only I'm not really. I want to know what I did wrong, so I don't do it again. I take a deep breath and brace myself before adding, "What's been up with you this week? Did I do something to upset you?"

Clench. Please don't hate me, please don't get defensive, please don't argue with me.

"God, no, Cooper! Sorry, I know I've been super crabby, I've just had stuff going on," she turns to face me, looking right into my eyes so I know she means it.

"What kind of stuff?" I ask before I can stop myself. Nosy bastard.

"Just stuff. I don't really want to talk about it. But it's nothing to do with you and I'm sorry if I upset you." She wraps an arm around my waist in a little half-hug and I relax into her. If she doesn't want to talk about it, I'm not pushing.

"As long as everything's okay," I tell her, awkwardly trying to wrap an arm back around her but knocking her elbow with my big spade hand.

"We're all good," she replies with a firm nod, letting go of me.

I deflate slowly as she walks away.

I meet her after school at the gates and we walk into town side by side. She talks a lot, and I listen. She's jumping from topic to topic so quickly I'm not sure I'm even keeping up properly.

"So then, Eric told the teacher to 'go to hell'. I couldn't believe it, my jaw hit the floor!" she exclaims.

I chuckle a little. I'd love to surprise Whisper with some kind of ballsy behaviour, but the day I tell a teacher to go to hell is the day pigs fly.

"Anyway, everyone was totally shocked except Laura, who laughed really loudly. She is such a bitch."

"She is," I agree wholeheartedly.

"Plus, you know she totally pads her bra," Whisper tells me in a conspiratorial voice, her eyebrows raised.

I go pink. "I didn't know that, actually."

"Seriously? You can totally tell. Her boobs look all lumpy after lunchtime."

"I don't look at her boobs enough to notice," I say. Whisper laughs. "Good!" She links her arm through mine like it's the reward for giving the right answer, and I gladly accept her little arm, giving her a little squeeze.

"So, there's this new museum exhibition in town, all about feminism. I really want to go. I think feminism is so important, don't you, Cooper?"

I'm still trying to keep up with the rapid conversation topic changes and mutter something in accordance. To be honest, I don't really know much about feminism at all. I want to say something worthwhile though, so I ask, "Is that the museum that did the local artists exhibition?" I read about it, they featured some guy from the year above who got into art school a whole year early because he was so talented. I can't even imagine my work being in a goddamn museum. I'd drop dead with joy.

"Mmmm, not sure," Whisper squints her eyes as though she's thinking real hard. "But I do really want to go to that feminism show. I think it would be so cool. Jack would probably say it's a load of bullshit," she sighs.

"Jack?"

"My stepdad."

"Jack isn't a feminist?" I ask in mock horror, my free hand on my heart.

Whisper snorts. "No. He's too 'traditional' he says. If he had his way, my mum would quit her job and just take care of him all day," she says.

"Doesn't sound too bad," I joke.

"Oi! None of that!" she nudges me with her elbow, but doesn't unlink arms with me. I grin. Then she's off on a new topic all-together.

"I want to get some new earrings to wear out. Maybe some big crosses or something? Not that I'm religious. Fuck religion, that's what I say. There's nobody looking out for any of us up there, we've gotta take care of ourselves, stand up for ourselves." She turns to look at me, grabbing my arm with a strange intensity. "You remember that, babe. Always take care of yourself, don't rely on anyone else or pray for anything to get better. Praying's a waste of time."

I nod at her, slightly bewildered. "I can't keep up with your brain," I tell her.

"Yeah, I know. I have a lot on my mind all the time," she laughs. "Oh, God. You're not religious are you?" she suddenly asks, looking at me with wide eyes.

"Nah," I tell her. "I've never prayed or anything. I think there's something nice about believing in more, but life is what it is. I could pray for God to make me happy, but he can't. Only I can make myself happy," I tell her. Because it's true. I could ask God to take away my anxiety but nothing would happen. But real life? Real life gives me medication and therapy and breathing exercises. That's what helps me.

"Hey, shall we get piercings today? I'm gonna get one, you can just come for moral support if you don't want one. I saw a girl who got the inside of her ear done right here, see here? It's called the tragus. I'm gonna do it," she says decisively, tugging at her ear cartilage with vigour.

I blink. It's a lot of work keeping up with her. It's almost like she's been building up over the past week of not speaking to me and is exploding all over the place now.

One thing's for sure. "There is no goddamn way I'm getting a piercing," I tell her. I tried weed and it was a no from me. If she thinks I'm letting some dude stab me through the ear with a needle she's on another planet. Knowing my luck it would get infected and they'd have to cut my ear off. Plus, my mum would kill me.

She shrugs and pulls me along by the wrist until we're outside a shop I've never noticed. It's painted black and has white doodle-style drawings outside, and a light-up sign that says Poison Ink.

"Whisper, this is a tattoo studio, what are you doing?" I ask, suddenly envisioning myself getting home with a Mike Tyson tattoo on my face and no explanation for my mother other than 'I did it to impress a girl.' At least Prince would appreciate the gesture (but only if I got laid).

"No, look, they do piercings too. See?" She jabs a finger at the price list framed and hung beside the door and I see that she's right. I relax slightly. No face tattoo today. My mother can rest easy.

Whisper pushes the door open and an automatic bell rings. I clench my hands once, swallow, and follow her in. It smells of incense and I notice a bundle of purple sticks burning beside the till.

The guy behind the counter is bald with a bushy beard, covered in tattoos, even on the inside of his ears. He has so many piercings around his mouth and lips that I imagine the sound of his cutlery clinking with the jewellery and shudder.

"You cold?" Whisper asks me, offering me her scarf.

"Nah," I reply, trying to play it cool.

The guy behind the counter lifts his head, sighs, and looks back down at the picture he's drawing. "ID please."

"We're only here for a piercing," she replies.

"Still need ID," he responds without looking up.

She makes a big show of rooting through her bag and then whines when she flicks through her purse.

"Look, mister. I've forgotten my ID, but I *swear* I'm sixteen. See, this is my twin brother, you can look at his ID if you want?" She pushes me up towards the counter and I start to feel sick. Why did she lie? I start feeling myself get itchy and my chest sucking itself in. I look up at him, my eyes bulging out of their sockets.

"You don't look like twins," the guy replies, slimming his eyes at me and setting his pencil down.

"Duh. We aren't identical. He's a *boy*." She rolls her eyes. "Go on, show him your licence," she gives me a nudge from behind. I pull my wallet out of my back pocket, my hand shaking slightly. I open it to my school ID which he scans with disinterest.

He doesn't seem to buy it but Whisper leans forward on the counter sticking out her breasts and twiddling her hair and eventually he glances up at a CCTV camera in the corner, sighs, and hands her a form to fill in.

I watch as she writes down Whisper Nelson at the top. I know she only did it because she told him we were siblings, but it still makes my gut twist.

I wonder how much trouble I can get into as an accomplice to this. This… what? Is it a crime? She's being voluntarily pierced, so surely it's not a crime? Unless it can count as identity fraud. Have I just committed identity fraud? I feel my hair sticking to my forehead and reach for a plastic cup, filling it from the water dispenser. I spill a little because my hand is shaking and try to pat it dry with my foot in a panic. It just smears into a bigger puddle and I try not to choke. Is the guy looking at me?

"Are you okay?" Whisper asks me, looking up from the book of tattoo designs she's flicking through.

I swallow. "Yeah."

I'm fine. I'm fine, I'm fine, I'm fine.

"Whisper Nelson, please." A girl with flowers tattooed on her forehead and a piercing on her wrist sticks her head out of a small private room, her hand on the door with an unwrapped needle in it's package.

Whisper stands, winking at me. "Let's go, bro!"

I follow her into the room to watch. I don't want to be left in the waiting room with the guy behind the counter. I feel a bit sick, but try to remind myself that Whisper must be feeling even more nervous. And she wanted me to be there for her, so I have to man up. That's what Prince would say.

The woman frets around, cleaning her ear with swabs that smell of alcohol and Whisper reaches over and takes my hand in hers. The piercer is speaking to us but I'm not listening, I'm just trying to work out exactly how clammy my hand is and how clammy Whisper's hand is and working out whether or not I should be mortified. I'm feeling hot and am praying to that God I don't believe in to stop me from sweating. I wish there was a water dispenser in here, too. She gives my hand a squeeze as though she's the one comforting me. I suddenly realise how strange this looks. The piercer probably thinks we're an incestual couple of siblings. I pull my hand away hastily, clearing my throat as I do so.

I turn and my eyes widen as the woman pulls out a super long needle from a bit of plastic and quickly pushes it through the hard bit of Whisper's ear. She doesn't even flinch, but I sure do.

"There we go, all done!" the piercer tells her, handing her a hand mirror. A bit of blood drips down from it. Whisper preens at her reflection, admiring the little diamond in her ear.

"Wow, I love it, thanks so much," she grins at the woman, who is already sticking her head out to check for any new customers.

"You were brave," I tell her as we walk out.

"I was born to be brave," she declares, punching her hand in the air. "Besides, this wasn't my first rodeo, cowboy." She smiles at me.

"What do you mean?"

"I have another piercing, but nobody knows about it," she tells me, her eyes doing the thing where they smile more than my mouth. "It's on my nipple. Want to see?" she asks.

I feel myself go so red I think I may legitimately pass out or something, my chest vibrates as my heart tries to jump out of my body. My mouth goes dry and she laughs at me.

"You're so cute, Cooper. You act like such a virgin sometimes."

I look at the floor. Being a virgin is so far down on the list of things I want to be discussing with Whisper. "Do your parents know about it?" I ask, trying to change the subject.

"My mam doesn't. She'd go mental if she knew! But my stepdad knows. I don't think he likes it," she replies with a casual shrug. "As if I care what he thinks."

"Your stepdad knows?" I repeat, my head snapping up. It strikes me as weird, and I get an uncomfortable feeling in my stomach.

She looks at me strangely. "Yeah, last summer I was in a bikini on holiday and he saw it through the fabric before I put a plaster on to hide it."

I nod, and drop the subject. Seems fair. I wonder what my parents would say if I got my nipple pierced, and then I smile to myself at how ridiculous I would look.

Half an hour in a tattoo and piercing parlour and I've come out imagining myself with a nipple piercing. I laugh out loud and Whisper looks at me curiously, but she's smiling too.

CHAPTER 6

THE VISIT

- **Remember asking me over for dinner?** Whisper texts me from across the classroom. I look up at her and she's looking at me with a playful glint in her eye.

- **Yeah...** I reply. As if I could forget.

- **Well, is it still on the cards? You haven't mentioned it again since.**

- **Neither have you. Yes it's on the cards.** What else could I say?!

- **Cool, because I wore my meet-the-mom outfit.**
I take in her long-sleeved black t-shirt, emblazoned with Venus symbol in pink on the front and grin.

- **You already have so much in common. Both females. Both crazy.**
I look up and she's grinning at my text. Then she looks over at me and sticks her tongue out, crossing her eyes. I laugh to myself. Then I text Mum.

- **My friend Whisper is coming for dinner tonight, is that ok?**
She replies instantly.

-Yes, of course! Oh gosh, what shall I cook? What does she like? Is she a vegetarian? What time will you get home? I need to clean now, why didn't you tell me earlier???

I sigh and put my phone away.

Two hours later I'm on a different emotional journey as I try not to barf. Nobody ever comes over other than Prince, and he barely counts. I can't concentrate on anything during my classes and my stomach starts to twist. Why did I ever think this was a good idea? How does everybody else deal with people just coming into their homes, entering their personal space? It seems so… intimate.

I get a text from Prince and fumble twice to unlock my phone because my thumb has suddenly detached from my hand and become a shaking mess.

- I'm gonna stop by tonight, want to meet the infamous Whisper. Dw, I won't stay long. Don't want to cramp your style my man.

I exhale, feeling a weight come off me. Having Prince there will probably actually make it easier. He's great at holding conversation, even if the topics are below-par. I should have thought to invite him myself. I text back a thumbs up emoji and shut my phone off, feeling a little less sick. I try to plan out how the evening will go in my head, and then decide against this method. It will only make me more anxious if something goes off-kilter or I find myself needing to improvise.

Eventually, the last bell rings, and I'm waiting outside the school with my hands in balls and eyes darting from head to head as students stream out. Finally, I catch sight of her black hair, today in two little buns at the top of her head, held in with little star clips. I wave over to her and immediately regret it. I probably looked stupid, flapping my big spade hands at her. Goddamnit.

She gives me a little wag of her fingers back and pushes her way over to me. "I'm excited to experience your daily bus journey," she says conversationally as we walk over to the extremely unexciting bus mentioned.

"This is said bus, in all its glory," I tell her, spreading my arms theatrically.

"Magnificent," she murmurs with an appreciative nod.

"Who's your girlfriend, Nelson?" Barfy Ben sniggers behind me.

My head combusts and I'm sure my veins all explode as I go the reddest I've ever gone in my life.

"Jealous, Barf-bag?" Whisper snipes back quickly. Sniggers from the rest of the crowd.

Barfy Ben looks to the floor and shuffles his feet, glaring at Whisper but saying nothing.

"How do you know about Barfy Ben?" I ask her, my voice low.

She winks at me and taps the side of her nose. Slowly, I feel my face regain its normal colour and mentally thank Whisper for being Whisper in that moment.

The bus door eventually opens and everyone streams on.

"Cooper!" Marvin greets with a nod. "And a lady friend," he adds with a grin, nodding again at Whisper who smiles sweetly at him.

"This is Whisper," I tell him, trying not to smile.

"Is it, now? Welcome to the west-side bus, Whisper," he tells her. When she starts to walk away, Marvin gives me a wink and I grin back.

She tugs on my sleeve as we sit down. "You're friends with the bus driver?"

"Marvin?" I say. "Yes, of course. He's picked me up and taken me home every day for the last five years. I think it would be a goddamn shame if we weren't friends after all that time."

Whisper looks at me in a peculiar way for a moment, then smiles to herself as the bus pulls away. "You're something else" she says.

The ride to my stop is uneventful. I watch Whisper out of the corner of my eye as she watches my neighbourhood blur by with childlike wonder that has me wishing I could peer into her thoughts. We walk to my house together after getting off the bus and she chats about how she hates the concept of veganism and then somehow this leads into a rant about terrorist cells. I have no clue how she linked these two topics together, but she did so quite gracefully and I can't help but be impressed.

I don't say much, if I opened my mouth, I feared I would be sick on myself. I spent the entire bus journey trying not to sweat in anticipation of all the things that could go wrong this evening. I look at my boring street and see it through her eyes, comparing it to how I imagine London to be. It's so dull and quaint, so quiet and boring. She stands out like stardust somewhere like this, and I'm the grey of the suburbs beside her.

"Babe, are you okay? You look kind of pale," she says, peering at me carefully.

I shrug. "Yeah, I'm fine." My tongue feels too fat for my mouth. She nods and carries on talking, because now she's discussing the feminist movement and how more men should be actively involved and I can't say anything because I'm so goddamn nervous suddenly. *Clench, unclench.*

As we approach my house, I see my mum waiting anxiously by the window, quickly darting behind the curtains when we come into view. She probably thought Whisper was going to blow me off. (The cancel-plans type of blow-off. Obviously.) I swallow as we approach the boring terraced house and fumble a little with the key. Whisper is still talking passionately about women's rights, kicking the floor around her and swinging her arms wildly. I have no idea what the hell she's saying.

I open the door and straight away Mum rushes over, fussing all over Whisper. "Oh dear, let me take your scarf for you. What lovely hair you have! I wish my hair was such a striking colour!"

Whisper seems to be enjoying all the attention and delves into a deep conversation about the hair dye she uses, Mum nodding along solemnly. I shuffle my feet awkwardly and hang my coat on the rack beside Whisper's.

"Let me get you a cup of tea, dear. Or would coffee be better?"

"Coffee please, black is fine," Whisper replies. This seems infinitely more mature than any choice I would make. Coffee tastes bitter and gives me the shits. Mum sets the kettle on and sets three mugs out, two with tea bags and one with a spoonful of instant coffee. I hope instant is okay.

We stand around awkwardly for a bit and Whisper eventually starts wandering around the kitchen, peering at things curiously. She sees the painting of Max on the fridge. "Wow, Cooper, this is amazing," she says, turning to look at me.

"It's fabulous isn't it?" Mum gushes. "I just can't wait to see how he develops when he goes off to art school."

I blush. I feel like I look like such a mummy's boy right now.

"You're going to art school?"

"I'd like to, eventually," I mumble.

Whisper nods as though making the decision for me. "I think that would be really good for you."

I see my mum's eyes start to shine as though she has just discovered that Whisper is a goddamn messiah and I decide now is the time to separate them. "Let's go upstairs," I say, making my way towards the stairs.

"Yes, you go have fun. I'll shout to you when dinner's ready," Mum says, handing us our mugs. "Oh, and Cooper? Leave the door open, dear," she tells me with a smile that says 'don't fuck with me' beneath the surface.

"Oh, don't worry Mrs Nelson, we'll keep it PG," Whisper says lightly.

Mum's smile fixes on her face for just a moment while she tries to work out whether Whisper is winding her up and she lets out a forced laugh. I smile to myself and lead Whisper up the stairs and into my room, doing a last minute mental inventory of any geeky things I may have out on display.

It suddenly seems very inadequate as far as bedrooms go. I sit on the edge of my bed like a nervous guest whilst Whisper fingers and examines every single object in my room, starting at my desk.

"What's this? What's that? Did you paint this? Why is this here? Do you use this? Where did you get this from?" She's so full of questions I can't keep up and I watch her playing with a rubix cube she found on my bookshelf absentmindedly whilst she scans my graphic novel collection.

"You know, these covers aren't very feminist-friendly," she tells me with a raised eyebrow, pulling out a book which has a woman drawn on the front in a very small dress.

I go red (no surprise there). It's not like I drew the goddamn cover. "I like the story."

"Huh. I've never read one of these. Maybe I can borrow one some time?" she asks, reading the back cover blurb.

"Sure, I can find one you'll like," I offer.

She places it back in it's place carefully and carries on walking around the room slowly, inspecting everything as she goes. I pick up the rubix cube that she's placed down on the bedside table and finish it for her.

When she turns to say something, she notices it and freezes, her mouth hanging open.

"Did you just finish that cube puzzle?" she asks me, her eyes wide.

"Er… yes?" I tell her.

"How?"

"There's a simple algorithm," I explain, moving the sides quickly to demonstrate. "See, if this is here, then you always move it like this." *Twist, twist, turn.* "And now this side is done."

"How did you learn to do that?" she asks, sitting beside me and taking it from my hands to inspect.

"I don't know, I just taught myself, I guess. It keeps my mind busy when I'm thinking too much about stuff."

"Maybe I should get one," she muses. Suddenly she looks at my hands and back up to me. "Why are your hands like that?"

"What?" I stammer. I try to pull them away but she's too quick, her little paws reaching out and grabbing my hands, unfurling my fingers to reveal my palms, bruised and marked from my constant clenching.

"Cooper, what is this?" she asks again, holding my hand up by the wrist and giving it a little shake.

I sigh and rip my hands from her vice-like grip. She's strong for someone so little. "It's nothing. I have a bad habit, I clench my hands a lot."

"You… clench your hands? Until they look like that?" she repeats, disbelieving.

"Yes?" I say.

"But that must hurt, surely?" I think of her cuts.

"I don't feel it," I tell her honestly.

She narrows her eyes at me but says nothing more. My hands itch to curl back into their tight little balls but I'm conscious of her noticing and force myself to lay them flat on the bed beside me. I feel embarrassed, and for some reason, ashamed.

She leans back a little against the wall and I feel my back stiffen like an ironing board and the rest of my muscles tense as if braced for some sort of attack.

She doesn't seem to notice though.

"Your mum's pretty cool," she says with a sigh.

"Yeah, she's okay," I reply.

"She really supports you. I think it's so cool that you want to be an artist and you've got everything all figured out. It would be pretty great, making money doing something you love. I have no clue what I want to do. Probably work in a brothel," she sighs again.

This shocks me so much that I gasp, and try to cover it up as a cough. Is she joking? I can't really tell.

"You can be anything you want to be Whisper. Don't drag yourself down like that."

"Do you think I'm attractive?" She looks at me and her eyes look so sad, so desperate. I decide to be brave one more time, because she deserves the truth.

"I think you're the most beautiful girl I have ever met," I tell her.

She gives me a small smile and looks at her lap where she's twisting her rings around her thin fingers. I'm not sure what to say, so I keep silent and still, waiting for her to say whatever it is she wants to say and wishing the goddamn door wasn't open.

"How come you've never tried anything with me?" she asks eventually, her voice quiet and washed with a timidness I've never seen from her before.

"I didn't know I was supposed to," I reply, honestly.

She lets out a small laugh.

"Do you want me to try something on you?" I add.

She looks at me and takes my head in both hands and smiles at me. For a moment I think she might be about to kiss me and my whole body turns into a statue, but then she lets go and my shoulders loosen, and my heart starts beating again.

I'm saved from trying to manoeuvre myself into a new topic of conversation because the doorbell rings, and then I hear Prince say, "Evening, Mrs Nelson. Hope it's okay I've stopped by?"

"No problem at all, Harry. Cooper and Whisper are upstairs, I have enough food for you if you would like some dinner?"

"That would be great," he replies, and I can hear his footsteps trampling up the stairs quickly.

He bursts into the room as though expecting to stumble upon a scene from 50 Shades of Grey and looks momentarily disappointed to see us both sitting beside each other on the bed with our hands in our laps. Then his eyes shine as he saunters over to Whisper and holds out his hand.

"Harry McGovern. You can call me Prince," he adds with a grin.

"Whisper," she responds primly.

"This is my best friend," I explain.

"I wanted to meet the girl sending Cooper doolally," Prince tells her with a wink.

If I had a gun, I swear to God I would shoot Prince right now.

She gives a small laugh. "Well, here I am."

He eyes her up and down theatrically, crossing his arms and frowning. "Satisfactory," he says finally. I can't help but break into a grin. The kid's got balls.

"Rude!" she retorts, throwing a cushion at him. He catches it and throws it back at us and suddenly we are embroiled in a full-on fight, Whisper standing behind me and clutching onto the waistband of my jeans squealing, "Protect me Cooper, protect me!"

I'm enjoying myself so much I don't even think about how potentially stressful and embarrassing the situation is, I'm just smacking Prince around the head with a pillow as he shouts and hollers, trying to reach the bed so he can arm himself.

"Goddamn, Cooper, I surrender dammit!" he shouts. I stop swinging the cushion and smile smugly, Whisper collapsing with laughter behind me.

"My hero," she says, bringing a hand to her forehead like a damsel in distress.

"Dinner!" Mum bellows from downstairs.

We all grin at each other as we hustle down the stairs to the table, which Mum has laid out as though it's the grandest event of the year. I notice Bella is out for the evening, but Dad's already sat at the end. He stands when Whisper walks in. "You must be Whisper! It's nice to meet you," he says.

"And you," she replies politely, twiddling her hands behind her back. She seems a little shyer around my dad than she was with my mum, but when we sit down, she quickly returns to her usual self.

"Prince, keep the food on your plate, fork, or mouth please," my dad warns, eyeing him comically.

"I make no promises," Prince replies, his hands in the air.

It's strange how naturally we all come together, how normal it feels having Whisper in our midst. I spent so long worrying about this, I wish I could go back in time and tell myself that it was all going to be fine. I wish this quite a lot, actually. But the thing is, no matter how much I tell myself that everything is going to be okay, my stomach still twists and turns and knots and my body tells me that no, it's not going to be alright. All I can do is enjoy moments like this to their fullest while they're here, my stomach calm. Apart from the little hunger pang. I'm starved!

Mum places a huge bowl of spaghetti bolognese in the middle and I eye it up greedily. "Don't be shy, now. Tuck in everyone," Mum invites.

"Ladies first," Dad says, piling Mum's plate up and reaching for Whispers.

"So, Whisper, Cooper says you're from London?" Mum asks conversationally.

She nods, her mouth full of food, then swallows. "Yep. Brixton area."

"And how are you finding it here?" Dad asks.

"It's okay. It's pretty quiet, there's not much to do. But now I've made friends with Cooper it's gotten better," she smiles. I feel my ears get hot.

"And Prince!" Prince pipes up.

"And, as of today, Prince," she corrects herself.

Prince wiggles in his chair, puffing his chest out.

Mum shifts in her seat and holds her chin out a little and I can tell she's glad I've made a new friend. A new friend that's a girl, nonetheless. A bit pathetic really, taking sixteen years to get to this stage.

"Yes, I suppose compared to London it is quite boring here," Dad agrees.

"Lovely countryside for walks though," Mum quips.

I roll my eyes. "We aren't ninety, Mum."

"You like going out with Max," she says defensively. I feel bad instantly, as though I was implying she was out of touch.

"Where is Max?" Whisper perks up.

"He's out back, we let him out during dinner time so he can't beg for food," Dad explains.

"You can meet him after," I tell her.

I look over at Prince and he has spaghetti sauce dribbling down his arm and I snort a laugh.

When dinner finishes Mum opens the back door and Max comes hurtling in, a mass of ears and feet. He bounds up to Prince first to greet him, then rushes over to the exciting new stranger, Whisper, who has gotten down on her knees and is squealing with delight.

"Max! Maxi! Are you a good boy? Yes, yes you are a good boy," she says, ruffling his forehead as he clambers all over her. She laughs in delight and we all stand around her in a circle, watching affectionately.

"Well, I'd better get going," she says wistfully, standing up and brushing the remnants of Max off her clothes. "My stepdad gets really upset if I'm home too late."

"Oh no! Do apologise if we've kept you too long. It's been so lovely having you, please come back any time," Mum tells her, fussing over her coat and fastening it up for her like she's a child.

"Thank you so much for having me! I really did have the best time," she says, and I swear she looked straight at me. "Better run, got to catch the next bus into town."

She gives me (and Prince) a quick goodbye hug and then she's gone. The house seems quieter as soon as she steps out the front door.

"Lovely girl," Mum says to herself.

Suddenly Prince explodes in a whoop, jumping in the air. "She's great, Cooper! Now, don't go ditching me for her or anything, bros before hoes - er, sorry Mrs Nelson - bros before girlyoes, but I like her." He nods as though giving me permission to be her friend.

I grin back, because he's right. She's great.

I go to sleep and for the first time in months, I don't get dizzy-head syndrome. I don't really think about anything other than how great the evening was and how there are potentially many more to come. Who would ever have thought it?

I'm woken hours later by a strange rapping on my window. I lay in bed, my eyes wide open. Then it happens again. Somebody is outside, deliberately rapping on my window.

My chest tightens and I whip my head around my room, looking for a potential weapon. I hurry to my wardrobe as the rap comes again, louder this time. I fumble in the dark and emerge wielding an old cricket bat from primary school, pulling the curtains back slowly, bat in hand.

The first thing I see is a little hand laden with chunky rings waving frantically.

Whisper is at my second-floor window. I blink in surprise and throw the curtains open all the way, revealing her pale face peering up at me. She spots the bat in my hand and mouths 'what the fuck?' at me. I quickly drop it, opening the window.

"What's with the bat, you freak?" she asks.

"*I'm* the freak? I thought you were a goddamn burglar," I hiss at her.

She giggles quietly. "A burglar who knocks?"

"Whisper, what are you doing? How the hell did you even get up here?" I ask, throwing my head out of the window and looking down.

"I climbed the trellis," she says, as though it's obvious.

"You climbed. My mum's. Rose trellis." I repeat slowly, rubbing my temples. I'm actually pretty impressed. It's high and the tread-space is thin, so she must have good footing. I wouldn't have been brave enough. I turn and she's stood in my room like a ninja, blinking at me in the darkness.

"So?" I ask.

"I was bored. Thought we could hang out," she says. She's trying to sound laid back, but her posture is a little stiffer than usual, her movements jerky. I glance at the clock. It's approaching 1am.

"You were bored." I repeat. "It's the middle of the night, you're not meant to be bored, you're meant to be asleep."

"It's not the middle of the night," she says with a sigh. "It's the beginning of the morning! The day has just begun, Nelson." She throws herself onto my bed with her arms open like a cross.

Once again, I stand awkwardly, feeling like a guest in my own bedroom. "Is something wrong?" I ask eventually.

"Nothing I want to talk about. I'm just here for the company," she says. She pats the bed. "Come and lie with me?"

I walk slowly over to the bed and carefully get in next to her, facing her so we can chat but careful not to touch her. My body is rigid, perhaps with fear, perhaps with discomfort, I'm not too sure. I've never been in this sort of situation before. I don't want to do the wrong thing, to accidentally brush against her and freak her out. I don't know how to lay, so I just try to stay as still as possible.

The curtains are still open and light from the streetlamps and moon are coming through the windows, running over her face like torchlight. Seeing her close-up, despite the darkness, I notice she doesn't have all the makeup she wears at school on and her black hair is more wild and free now, like a small lion's mane. Her eyes are still the brightest blue I've ever seen, but they aren't coated and rimmed in black anymore, so they look smaller and more youthful. She has freckles too, which I hadn't seen before, running across her cheeks and over her nose like a bridge. She looks different, but the same. The nose stud is still in and she's wearing the same smile as always. She's so beautiful.

"I'm really glad we're friends," she tells me in a hushed tone.

"So am I. You're the only friend I have at school," I admit.

"You've never had a friend at Bennessons before?" she asks. She sounds a little shocked and I have to 'shh' her because I don't want my parents to wake up. She mumbles, "sorry".

"Not one who comes to my house and hangs out with me like Prince. Because I'm awkward. But I'm getting better," I tell her. And when I think about it, it's true. Even in the last couple of weeks I've been more sociable and 'normal' than I've been in years. It's almost as though she's fixing me.

She looks at me with her icy eyes and they are drowning in sadness. I don't know whether the sadness is her own, or pity for me.

"What about you?" I ask, trying to move the subject away from how pathetic I am.

"What about me?"

"Why did you come here tonight? Surely you have a ton of friends you could go to?" She's so cool and confident and interesting, I can't understand why I, Cooper Nelson, would be her first choice for a late-night chat.

I feel her shift beside me and I can tell she was trying to shrug. "Not really. I don't speak much to the girls from my last school anymore, we were never that close. I don't know many people around here yet."

So she's lonely. And she chose me for company, for a friend. I can't believe my goddamn luck.

"So, you've never had a girlfriend before either?" she asks.

I blink and swallow. "What?"

"You said that you haven't really had many friends. Does that mean you haven't had a girlfriend before, too?

I consider lying, making someone up, a holiday romance with a wild Spanish girl called Rosaria or something. Anything so she doesn't realise I'm such a sad case. But instead I just shake my head. "I haven't really spoken much to girls before you. Not since primary school time I guess. Have you had boyfriends?"

Of course she's had boyfriends.

"Nope," she shakes her head violently and now it's my turn to be surprised.

"I don't trust any boys. Other than you, obviously. I don't want a boyfriend. I don't want to have to make my life about another person."

I'd never thought of it like that, as a sacrifice. It almost makes me upset for her, that she is so cynical about love that it's a negative thought for her. I think about this for a while and we lay in silence for a bit. Eventually I reply, "I think when you really love someone, it isn't a chore to make your life about them. You just want to incorporate them in every way possible because you enjoy spending time with them."

I think this is a bloody romantic speech, but she grunts noncommittally, which makes me smile. She isn't like any other girl, she never does what I expect her to.

We lay in a comfortable silence again and it drags on for so long that I almost drift to sleep, because my body has relaxed and isn't tense and uncomfortable any more. She nudges me to check I'm still awake and I make a small noise to indicate that I am, but that I don't really want to chat. I'm so tired.

"Cooper? Could you maybe sleep with your arms around me?" she asks quietly.

"If you want me to," I reply.

She turns so her back is facing me and I put my arms around her, so I'm holding her tightly.

"Thanks," she whispers softly.

I feel her entire body against mine and her warm breaths on my forearm. I become tense again.

"Your heart is beating fast," she murmurs, sleep trickling into her voice.

"Sorry," I mumble.

I feel Whisper's body go limp and hear her whispy breaths get longer and deeper and I know she's fallen asleep. I begin to worry about what I'll do in the morning about my parents, but for once I make the conscious decision to worry about it later and to enjoy every minute of this moment.

I, Cooper Nelson, have the most beautiful girl in my arms, fast asleep next to me. I feel like everything will be okay for now, and I feel the calmest I've felt in a long time.

CHAPTER 7

NOT A DATE

I barely slept all night. I wanted to stay awake and relish the moment of having Whisper asleep beside me, but my body disagreed and I nodded off a few times. The morning inevitably came, sun streaming through the window at a godforsaken hour of 6am. She didn't stir and had pillow marks across her face creating a strange pattern of indentations, like map lines sitting against her ghostly complexion.

I try to sit up slowly, and she groans in complaint.

"Whisper?" I give her an experimental nudge. "It's morning, you have to leave."

She rubs her eyes and sits up, stretching and making a strange sound like a cat. "Oh Jesus, it's morning. I have to get home before my parents check my room or I'm in so much trouble. My stepdad will freak out and ground me for sure." She jumps out from under the covers and scurries over to the window, yanking down at the latch. "See you at school," she whispers. As quick as a blink she's out of the window, scaling back down the wall. I watch her running down the road and know I won't get back to sleep, so I sit at my desk and sketch.

I don't even pay attention as I draw, my hand moving without thought across the page as though completely disconnected from my mind. Is this what they mean when they say girls make you go crazy? Literally, can't-control-my-own-limbs crazy?

Am I going to look down and see a page of psychotic murder-related doodles, Patrick-Batemen-American-Psycho-style?

I look down. I've drawn mountains. They're pretty damn good actually.

I text Prince as I head up to the front doors of school.

- Whisper snuck back last night and stayed round! And no, nothing untoward occurred. *eye roll emoji.*

His reply: **- Get in!!!**

The afternoon is P.E, my least favourite class because I'm useless. I'm uncoordinated, weak, and my body seems to just do its own thing rather than what I want it to. Nobody ever wants me in their team, and I struggle through the entire class while people laugh at me, which makes it a very unenjoyable two hours of the day. So when Whisper texts me and asks if I want to bunk off with her, I say yes. When you've done it once before, it seems to get easier to repeat without feeling too guilty.

I write a phoney note from my mum saying I have a bad ankle and limp over to my P.E teacher, Mr Bryce. Mr Bryce knows I hate his class, but he tries as hard as he can to get me involved. I never bunk off, so he doesn't suspect anything when he scans the note. Usually if you're unable to join the class you still have to sit in at the sidelines, but I ask if I can catch up on some homework and he lets me. I like Mr Bryce and feel bad about being deceitful, but I really want to spend the two hours with Whisper instead of panting around a field, sweating like the Amazon River and getting yelled at by everybody for doing the wrong thing.

I meet her by the bench behind the school again. For some reason I feel awkward, like I can't look her in the eye. I'm worried she regrets coming over last night, that she went home and thought things over and realised how lame I am.

"So I got home and my parents didn't suspect a thing. Thank God."

"That's good. Mine, too," I tell her, relieved that she's acting normal. Plus, the last thing I would need would be an irate Mrs Whisper calling my mum up to reveal our Rated U late-night antics.

As we walk through the park she chats away and I listen, all the while wondering how it could be that she has no friends. I understand why I don't have friends, but she's the total opposite of me in every way. She should be dripping friends.

"I'm so glad I didn't get caught. Last time I was grounded it was for skipping school and Jack took my phone away for two whole weeks! I'm sure he was reading any messages I got in that time as well, the psycho," she says.

"That sucks," I tell her supportively.

We end up back at our spot by the banks and trees. She didn't fake a note, she just didn't bother turning up.

"Won't you get in trouble? What if you get grounded again?" I don't want her to lose her phone, then she won't be able to text me anymore.

"Nah, my parents aren't home, and the school doesn't have their mobile numbers. They work long hours, I'll delete any voicemail messages before they get home," she says casually.

How much do her parents even know about her? Do they know about her arms? They must, it's not like she tries particularly hard to hide them. Maybe that's the real reason they moved her out here - to try to help her.

My thoughts are interrupted when I get a serious case of déjà vu as she pulls out the same sparkly unicorn lighter and starts to build a joint. I'm about to turn it down when I get a sudden surge of determination. It's like all of a sudden, I *want* to smoke it, to prove to myself that I can do things that are so far out of my comfort zone and not wimp out. I decide this time to smoke a little bit more than last time, as nothing really bad happened and I want to try and see all the animals Whisper can see in the clouds. More than that, I want to start experiencing stuff. Normal stuff, that all the other kids do at school. I don't want to be afraid to try new things all the time, and having Whisper here with me makes me feel like I can be brave enough to try things. Even if they're the type of things my mother would kill me over.

The first breath I take is better than last time. I'm prepared for what to expect and manage not to cough. It tastes rank, but I deal with it, my eyes watering and throat stinging a little.

"The rule is puff, puff, pass," she tells me. I take another puff and hand it over to her.

Puff, puff, pass. Puff, puff, pass. Over and over until it's all gone, and my mouth feels sticky and dry. So, I've had approximately half of this joint. Now what?

We sit back and I wrap my coat around myself a little tighter. The air is dry, but crisp with a chill.

Eventually I start to feel very lethargic and heavy, as though time is moving very, very slowly. I watch the leaves of the trees in the breeze and they seem to curl slowly as they blow in the wind, twisting like snakes. Beneath my hands the grass feels so cold and hard, but also like hay. I move my hands slowly between the blades of grass and it feels so intense for some reason. It feels like we've been lying there at least an hour, but when I check my watch it's been five minutes. Only five minutes? How is that even possible?

"Whisper, it's only been five minutes," I tell her, my mouth tacky.

"So?"

"So, it feels like it's been an hour." My mouth moves slowly, and my tongue feels heavy.

She laughs. "You're just high, Nelson. Revel in it," she says, blinking in slow motion. I want to clench my hands but my fingers just twitch, the muscles too relaxed to curl into a proper fist.

We lay in silence and I can feel the breeze brushing my face and watch wisps of her dark hair dance with it. She's lying with her arms above her head and I look at all the tiny scars which lace up to her elbow. Most are white and faded, some look slightly newer. All of them look painful.

"Stop looking," she says. She hadn't turned her head or her eyes, so she must have felt me staring in her peripheral vision.

"Sorry," I mumble.

"They're hideous. They make me look damaged." She rolls her sleeves down and turns away so I can't see her face anymore.

I'm not sure what to do so I sidle closer and put my arms around her like we had that night in my bed. I'm hoping it makes her feel better again.

"You're not damaged," I tell her. She moves her head a little bit and clasps my arms so I can't let go of her. My arms feel so heavy it's as though they are tied around her by invisible chains.

"Well I am," she mutters.

I think about this for what feels like a long while, before sighing. "Perhaps you're just a little broken, but the kind of broken you can fix with a bit of tape or glue. But you aren't damaged to the point of being worthless or something to throw away," I say, thinking hard. In my head this sounds extremely philosophical, like I have just cracked The Meaning Of Life. In reality, I'm just stoned.

She is quiet for a long time, and I'm not sure she understands what I was trying to say. So I tell her, "I'll try to be your glue so you don't feel broken any more." And then she turns and hugs me, really, really tightly.

When she pulls away my coat is wet and her black eyes are smudged underneath because she's crying and I don't know why she's crying or what I can do about it. I just let her lie next to me with her face burrowed into my chest and with extreme concentration I lift my weighty arm and place a hand on her head because it seems like the right thing to do. I read once that stroking or holding the back of the head is comforting because it's linked with memories of being an infant held by your mother. So I do it, to comfort her. And I guess it works, because after a while she stops crying.

I'm not sure how long she'd been crying for. It felt like a long time, but it was probably only a few minutes.

When I'm susare she's stopped, I point to the sky and I say, "Look, a rabbit on a broomstick."

She laughs.

I text Whisper later that evening. I don't mention her crying, I don't imagine she's forgotten and if she wanted to speak about it she would bring it up. My hands haven't clenched all day and feel oddly achy. I can't remember the last time they had remained loose by my sides for this long. Despite this, I tap out my text conclusively.

- Whisper, I am not smoking weed ever again. I hope this won't change anything between us. It's just not my thing.

She responds immediately. **- I don't mind. :)**

I let out a sigh of relief. The thing is, I kind of goddamn hated it. I hated the smell, the way it made my mouth taste and my throat feel. I hated the way it made me feel so tired and exhausted that I couldn't move. I hated how I felt like I had to hide it. Most of all, I hated how it felt like it was always somehow restricting me. It was restricting my anxiety, but it was also slowing my brain down, restricting all my thoughts. And at the end of the day, aren't we all just the sum of our thoughts?

**

On Friday, I surprise Whisper with tickets to the museum exhibition in town she had been speaking about the other week. I don't feel anxious like I did before giving her the painting, because I know for sure she will like this gift. I bought it mostly to cheer her up, but also because I like going to museums. I haven't been to one in years, but I find them calm and relaxing, like libraries. It's not a date, per-se, but it's a chance to spend more time getting to know her outside the confines of our school.

I wield the tickets in her face as soon as I see her. She frowns at them in confusion and then realises what they are. She leaps into the air and shouts, "Yes!" and throws her arms around me.

People are looking over because of the commotion but I grin stupidly because I don't mind people staring at me when Whisper has her arms around me.

"This is so great, will we go tomorrow?" she asks, taking the ticket and turning it over to read the small print.

"Sure, it's valid all weekend," I tell her.

The exhibition is called *History of the Feminist Revolution*, so if I'm being honest it wouldn't have been my first choice of how to spend my Saturday. But I knew she'd love it and she makes anything seem fun, so I thought, sod it, and bought her the tickets. And seeing the smile on her face, I'm glad I did. Her eyes are shining, her dimples appearing, and I know that it's all for me. And with that smile, I am hers.

Saturday morning I allow myself a luxurious lie-in, getting out of bed at 9am. I bite my lip as I inspect my wardrobe offering, rubbing the back of my head. The most I do at weekends is play videogames with Prince or watch him smoke out of my window, neither of which require choosing a presentable off-duty weekend outfit. It's not the same as dressing for school, you're less restricted by social ties. I highly doubt a stranger is going to make fun of my outfit at the museum. But what if they do? What if we bump into someone we know there?

I resist the urge to clench my hands and take a deep breath to calm myself. I can do this. I can do this. I can do this.

I frown at the selection again and eventually reach for a pair of black kind-of-skinny-kind-of-straight jeans. You can't go wrong with black jeans. Everything goes with black jeans. I pick up a buttoned shirt. I put it back down. I pick it up once more. Too try-hard, too formal. I put it back down. I reach for a sweatshirt with a Fortnite reference on the front. Too casual. And geeky. I put it back down. I put the jeans back in the wardrobe. I take them out again. I consider smashing my head through the wall.

I pick up a knitted grey crew jumper, throw it onto my bed alongside the black jeans and shut the wardrobe door before I can change my mind again.

I decide I need a coffee before I attempt to navigate the minefield that is my shoe collection.

I head downstairs and get my Marmite out of the fridge, dropping bread into the toaster on my way to the kettle which I set on.

"Why are you up so late?"

I jump and turn around to find Bella in her fluffy grey dressing gown and monstrous pink rabbit slippers. She has her glasses on and no makeup and is opening a box of potato waffles and throwing them under the grill. She looks like she hasn't slept.

"It's not late, it's ten o'clock. And I'm going to a museum."

She pauses and looks at me over her specs. "You're going to a museum?" she repeats, wrinkling her nose and frowning.

"Yes, that's what I said."

"What museum? Who are you going with?"

"I'm going to The Barkley Museum with Whisper."

She raises one perfectly groomed eyebrow. "Like a date?"

I go red. "No, not like a date. Like an *activity*."

She slowly grins, her eyes lighting up like a cat that's just cornered a mouse. She could hear the desperation in my denial. "It is a date! It's a date, you're going on a date!" She runs over and starts ruffling my hair while I slap her away.

"Get off me! It's not a goddamn date!"

I collect myself and spread the Marmite onto my toast and take what I hope is a nonchalant sip of my coffee, pretending I can't feel her staring at me.

"Is that what you're wearing?" she pulls a face.

Automatically, I clench my hands and unclench, tugging at the hem of my jumper. "What's wrong with it?"

"Cooper, calm down. I'm joking. You look good. Throw on some white trainers and you're good to go." She gives me an approving nod and I roll my eyes. Inside, I'm glad. If Bella thinks I look good, it's as much as I can hope to achieve today. And she has just unknowingly solved my footwear dilemma.

I turn to head back upstairs with my plate and mug in hand.

"Hey, Cooper?"

I turn to look at her.

"Don't forget to pack a condom." She winks and sticks her tongue out.

"Urgh! You're disgusting! And I told you already, It's. not. a. DATE!"

I storm up the stairs and can hear her screeching with laughter in the kitchen as I slam my bedroom door.

I put on the white trainers and inspect myself in the mirror. To be fair, I do look pretty good. The trainers work. Damn Bella.

It takes another thirty minutes to sort out my hair and resist the temptation to pop a spot on my chin which will apparently be accompanying me.

Then I sit on my bed and my knee jumps up and down while I wait for her to arrive.

What if she doesn't come? What if she changed her mind? I'll be humiliated. My chest tightens immediately, as soon as the thoughts enter my head. I suck in a sharp breath and close my eyes. Be rational. She will come. You won't be humiliated. I begin counting backwards from ten until my heart rate slows down and I unclench my hands.

This is why I never do anything on the weekend. I remember now. Making plans is never worth the anxiety of going through with them.

The doorbell rings and my head snaps up, my eyes wide. She came. Panic over. No embarrassment to be had, no pitiful words from Bella, no painful rejection to fall asleep to. I hurtle down the stairs, almost knocking Bella over in the hallway.

"Whoa, chill out. That is not how you play it cool on a date," she says.

"It's not a *date*," I hiss back before opening the door. Whisper stands on the other side wearing a black puffer coat fastened up to her face, black tights and her little leather boots. She's wearing red lipstick and smiles at me in greeting. No lipstick on the teeth. She truly is a marvel.

"Cooper? Cooper is Whisper here?" I hear Mum call from upstairs in her bedroom.

"Hi," I mumble at Whisper as she wipes her feet on the door mat. Behind me Bella is leaning right over the upstairs banister and eyeing Whisper with interest. I try to pretend she isn't there. Moments later, Mum appears from her bedroom door. She rushes down the stairs, beaming.

"Whisper! I thought I heard the door. So lovely to see you again. Do you want a cup of tea or anything before you both head off? Oh no! It was coffee you drank. Silly me, coffee, perhaps?"

"No thank you, I just had one before I left," she smiles.

"Okay then," she turns to me. "Well if there are any problems give me a call, dear. Here's twenty pounds, get yourself both a nice lunch," she says, pushing a note into my hand.

"Thanks, Mum," I give her a kiss on the cheek, and she waves us both goodbye, Bella still watching with fascination.

We have to catch the bus from my street into the town centre where the museum is, which I usually hate. The bus stop is only a minute up the road but I get stressed on them, thinking about how many people have sat where I'm sitting, what they might have been touching, who might get on next, what they might say to me…. the list of concerns is endless. I try not to worry too much as we wait at the bus stop though. I want today to be a good day.

Whisper chews her gum loudly, popping bubbles every now and again and swinging her legs as she sits on the bus bench.

"Did you do anything last night?" I ask her.

"Not really. My stepdad was out, so me and my mum watched a film. We don't really hang out just the two of us anymore. We watched the second Bridget Jones film, it was hilarious," she tells me.

"I haven't seen it," I reply.

She shrugs. "Do you hang out with your family much?" She looks up look at me, her big blue eyes focussed on my expression, as though my response really matters. She makes me feel like the most important person in the world with that single look.

I consider the question, tilting my mouth. "Not really. Mum makes us all sit down for dinner together, but other than that we don't all have much in common."

"They seem nice though," she says, a hint of wistfulness in her voice. I'm about to ask more about her own family when the bus turns around the corner and she thrusts her hand out into the road, flagging it down. We get on and I head towards the back where there are empty seats. She grabs my arm and pulls me away. I look at her quizzically.

"Never sit on the back seats. It's where drunk people do dirty deeds after nights out," she says with a knowing look. I try not to gag, try not to recollect every single time I sat down in the back seats. Try not to imagine what I was touching and what I touched after. I make a mental note to

___

begin carrying anti-bac with me and sit down next to the window with a shudder, Whisper shimmying in beside me.

"So, you're saying there could potentially be old semen on the seats?" I ask in a low voice.

"Yeah, sure. Why not? Who knows what else might be on them?" She spits her gum out into a wrapper and pulls out her ipod, offering me a bud which I accept, keen to block out the thoughts of what my hands have potentially touched unwittingly throughout my lifetime of bus journeys.

She's playing Champagne Supernova by Oasis, her heart-shaped mouth slowly lip-syncing the lyrics.

I look out of the window at the trees passing by in a mix of orange and brown blurs, the houses grey and sad as the lyrics dance through the headphone.

With her sat beside me in a companionable silence and the music tying us both together, I find myself feeling calm and unafraid. The goddamn semen story is bothering me, of course, but not enough to make me need to throw up. I'm not worrying about who may or may not get on at the next stop. After all, what's the worst that could happen?

CHAPTER 8

CATFIGHT

We approach the museum, which is a refurbished town hall building with great columns outside and banners hung up announcing the launch of the new exhibition. I didn't realise it was such a big deal, but it looks pretty busy.

"I haven't been here since I was a kid," I tell Whisper.

"Well, it's my first time ever, so you'll have to show me all the best bits," she says, snapping a photo of the exterior on her phone, her tongue poking out the side of her mouth as she concentrates.

"I doubt I even remember all the best bits," I tell her. "I came with the school when they had a space exhibition. It must be all different now."

"Here, let's take a selfie," she says, pulling me in beside her and grinning for the camera. I give a lopsided smile but just look awkward and stiff beside her. I never manage to just look comfortable.

"I love it," she announces, sending me a copy.

I forward it to Prince so he thinks I have at least a bit of game.

- **Where was my invite??**
- **Next time**, I reply.
- **You sly old dog.**

I grin at my phone and tuck it back into my pocket. If I'm being honest, I didn't tell Prince about today to save myself from the embarrassment if she didn't turn up.

I hand our tickets over at the door and have no idea where to start. The building is huge with high ceilings and big pillars, notices pinned by the door and signs everywhere pointing towards different themes and rooms. Whisper isn't phased by the plethora of options and goes charging ahead up a winding staircase, her little legs moving surprisingly quickly. She stops halfway and turns to me. "Come on, Cooper!" she flaps her hand at me, and I follow, running a little to catch up with her.

When I reach the top (ashamed to admit, I'm a little out of breath), she's already gazing up at a huge print of women holding up a sign that says Votes For Women.

Her eyes are running down the photo drinking in every detail and I join her, standing quietly beside her and looking up at it blankly.

"Can you imagine, living in a time when women had no right to vote? Like we weren't even real people?" she says.

I'm not sure if it's rhetorical or not. Either way I would have been on the better end of things, being a man and all, so I don't say anything. I feel awkward in situations like this, as though my birth has afforded me a privilege which means I don't deserve to comment on such matters.

"As if women aren't as good as men," she snorts as an afterthought.

A woman closeby starts nodding sympathetically and I feel like the ignorant male in a sea full of female fish. We sidle on ahead and look at more photographs, many of them accompanied by handwritten letters from the same era.

She reads them all carefully, every now and again shaking her head in a passionate way. I love the way she frowns thoughtfully, the way she is so curious, so empathetic, so lovely. I love the way she wants to take in every detail as if she can never come back. I love how she starts conversations up fearlessly with fellow onlookers. I love how she is so feisty, so fiery and fierce. She is like a powerful force of energy, and it would be a dishonour to miss a second of her passion. So I follow her around loyally, nodding along to her monologues.

As we continue around the room everything becomes more modern and I find myself getting into it all a bit more. The black and white historical photographs weren't really my thing, but there's a whole wall of pop-art style prints and posters which are pretty awesome.

There are whole charities devoted to making certain workplaces more equal, like technology, where they will teach women to code so they can keep up in a male-dominated environment, which is pretty cool. I feel intimidated just being in this museum filled with women, I can only imagine what it's like going into work every day and being surrounded by the opposite sex.

By the time Whisper is satisfied that she has screened every inch of the exhibition and that we are done for the day, I feel pretty ashamed of my penis privilege, and decide to be more consciously feminist whenever possible.

"What did you think?" she asks me, looking into my eyes as though my response actually matters.

"It was a big learning curve. I definitely didn't appreciate how much women struggled back in those days," I admit.

"Yeah. I really enjoyed it though, thanks so much for bringing me," she says, hooking her hand through my arm.

We step outside and I start to walk back to the bus stop, but she stops.

"Actually, my house isn't far from here. It's only about a fifteen minute walk that way, I was by your house this morning because I stayed at Ellie's last night," she explains, nodding in the opposite direction to the bus stop but remaining rooted in the spot, looking at me.

"I can walk you home," I offer.

"That's very gentlemanly," she smiles, "but you really don't have to." She's smiling in a way that I know she wants me to.

"Whisper, I know you're a strong, independent woman who can walk herself home, but I'd like to," I insist, already turning to follow her.

"You learn quickly, grasshopper," she grins.

We walk through town and she chats about the exhibition, her favourite parts (the suffragette photo displays) and her least-favourite (the hygiene standard in the ladies' toilets). I don't even realise we've reached her house until she stops by the gate. It's a detached house with its own driveway, but it's not huge or anything. A normal, suburban home. "Well, this is me, thanks for walking me back - although you really didn't have to."

"No problem. I'll see you next week," I reply.

I'm about to turn to leave when the front door swings open. "Whisper, you're home! And you must be Cooper?"

She knows who I am? I wonder what Whisper's told her about me. Her mum looks just like her. She's small, wearing a baggy oversized jumper, skinny jeans and fuzzy socks. She has the same delicate features, but her hair is a sandy blonde, and there are the beginnings of crow's lines on her face.

"Yes, it's lovely to meet you," I manage, walking up to shake her hand. I'm glad this was an impromptu meeting; I would have vomited with nerves if I had known I would be meeting a parent today.

"Come in, come in. Let me make you a cup of tea," she says, ushering me into the hall.

"Mum, Cooper has a home to get back to as well, you know," Whisper huffs.

I suddenly feel awkward, like I've intruded or overstepped the mark. Whisper probably doesn't even want me here.

"Yes, really don't worry about me. I was going to head home for dinner anyway," I explain.

"Did someone say dinner?" A head pops around the corner and Whisper recoils, cringing. This must be her step-father. He is startlingly unlike her, the opposite in almost every way. Blonde hair and olive skin with dark eyes, all very clean-cut, almost in a way that he looks like a wax model. He grins at me, extending a hand. "Hello," he says.

"Hello, sir. I'm Cooper," I shake his hand firmly, so he thinks I'm more confident than I am.

"Please, call me Jack. So, you're staying for dinner I understand?" He's disconcertingly charming.

"I, er..." I start stuttering as he winks at me.

121

"Yes, please do, I insist." Whisper's mum is now ushering me towards the living room, flapping her hands. "Food'll be ready in about half an hour," she nods firmly at me.

Whisper is pouting and curls up on an armchair, clinging onto a cushion.

"Thank you very much, it's very kind of you," I tell them.

Her mum disappears around the corner and then her voice rings through. "Jack, where did you put the blender?"

He pulls a dramatic wince. "Oops. I'd better go remember where I left that thing," he says, leaving the room quickly.

"I'm so sorry you have to sit through this. It's not too late, you can still sneak out and I'll tell them you got sick or something," she whispers to me quickly.

"Why would I do that? Your parents seem really nice," I tell her.

"He's not my parent," she corrects me sharply.

"Explains why you look nothing alike," I say with a nod.

She wrinkles her nose at me and then sighs and switches the tv on. "Oh my God, Catfish is on. I love this show," she says, turning the volume up. "I find this show so crazy, like how can it be real life? It's hard enough falling in love with people you *do* know, let alone with total strangers you've never even met."

I've never watched it before but, somehow, I'm sucked in and twenty minutes later we're being called for dinner and I've spent my entire time in this house watching a girl who thinks she's been speaking to a hot model called Jacob for the last five years only to discover that he is actually a chubby eighteen year old girl called Amanda. Fascinating.

The smell wafting through the house from the kitchen is delectable. I find myself sat at the table opposite Whisper with a plateful of roast chicken, spuds and veg, eyeing it greedily.

"We like to make dinner an event at the weekends as we usually can't eat together during the week," Jack explains, helping himself to some chicken.

"Why not?" I ask, waiting with my hands on my lap to begin eating. When Whisper digs in without question, I follow suit. Delicious.

"Mum's a nurse," Whisper replies.

"Oh. So you work night shifts?" I ask.

"Unfortunately so!"

"Well, the food is delicious," I say, keen to keep the conversation light.

"Thank you!" she lights up, as though I've offered to give her a spare kidney.

"Lana's food is always incredible," Jack gushes.

I notice Whisper point a finger into her mouth and pretend to vomit. If Jack or Lana noticed, they don't react.

"So, Cooper, we hear you're an artist?" Lana asks, and my head snaps up.

"Oh, I don't know. I like to mess about -"

"-Now don't you downplay it," Jack interrupts. "We saw the drawing you made Whisper, it was really something!" He's smiling but it looks like he's gritting his teeth and I shift uncomfortably.

"Yes, really wonderful!" Lana smiles and nods.

"Thanks," I mumble, looking at my plate.

"I hung it on the wall in my bedroom," Whisper explains. I look up to meet her gaze and she's smiling encouragingly, so my shoulders relax a little. I'm flattered.

"You looking at art schools?" Jack asks, leaning forward as though I'm really interesting.

"I've started to look, sir," I reply.

"Please, call me Jack," he smiles at me again with those commercial-fresh teeth. "Well, one of my buddy's at work, his sister is a professor at the London College of Art, I can ask for a reference or something if you'd like?" He's gone back to his knife and fork now.

My heart does a little jump of excitement at the prospect of a professor at the LCA seeing my work. "God, I'd love that. Are you sure?" I stammer, my eyes wide.

"For Whisper's friend? Not a problem," Jack grins and winks at me.

I glance over at Whisper and she rolls her eyes at me. I find it difficult to see why she hates him so much, he seems so goddamn *nice.*

After more small-talk and answering questions about my family, I finally admit I really should head home.

"Gosh, yes, we've kept you. So sorry, please apologise to your parents for me," Lana says.

"No, no. Thank you for having me," I say, tipping my head.

"I'll take him to the door," Whisper offers, leading me out. I give a little wave to Lana and Jack yells, "see you again soon," from the kitchen table.

"See you next week," Whisper says quietly.

"Next week," I confirm, opening the gate at the end of her drive and walking home with a smile plastered on my face.

***

"So, is she your girlfriend yet or what?" Prince asks, blowing a stream of smoke out of my bedroom window.

"She's not my girlfriend."

"Why not? If I had a friend that hot, I'd sure be working on making her my girlfriend," he says, as though I would actually have a shred of hope of ever making Whisper my girlfriend.

"It's not like that. We just hang out. She doesn't seem to be interested in having a boyfriend, anyway," I tell him.

"Whatever." He stubs his cigarette out on my window ledge and puts it in the empty plant pot which I placed out there as his designated fag-butt-pot. "So, you spent an entire day at the museum together, went to hers for dinner, did the whole meet-the-parents charade and you're telling me nothing even remotely romantic was going on behind the scenes?" He raises an eyebrow at me, closing the window and slumping onto my desk chair, spinning around on it lazily.

"Stop that. You're making me dizzy. And yes, that's exactly what I'm saying. It's completely platonic."

"Riiight," he says in a tone which implies he believes approximately 0% of my story. "At least now you know where she lives you can level out the playing field." He waggles his eyebrows dramatically.

I frown. "What playing field?"

"You know. She knocks on your window, you knock on hers…"

"I am not going to knock on her window," I tell him bluntly.

"Why not? She'd love it."

"She would?" I imagine it being creepy, but I suppose if I

think about it, I didn't find it creepy when she did it to me. I liked that she had turned up. Does that mean she would like it if I turned up?

"Yeah man, for sure. Turn up and surprise her, give her some flowers or some shit. Girls love that."

"Maybe… her mum does work night shifts…" I think out loud, unconvinced.

"There you go! That's a bloody sign," Prince says, standing up with excitement.

"Her stepdad would be home though," I argue.

"Yeah, but you can deal with avoiding just one parent. He'll be asleep anyway. Trust me, it's a great idea," Prince says.

"I'll think about it," I say grudgingly. What I mean is, I'll worry about it and probably not go through with it. But I know if I tell him I'll think about it, that he'll shut up for a while.

"Sweet. Also, there's a party next week in the woods behind Ben McGregor's house. You know, the big one at the end of Newton?"

Newton Street is one of the most expensive streets in town, and Ben McGregor goes to PTS where he is unbelievably snobby and arrogant, even by their standards. But he throws great parties in the woods behind his house, so everyone puts up with him. I know this because Prince keeps me in the loop, not because I go to parties.

"Cool," I respond.
"You should come. With Whisper," he adds, looking at me eagerly.

"I don't do parties, you know that," I sigh, leaning back on the bed.

"You didn't *used* to do parties. You've changed since you met Whisper, you're way more outgoing," he says.

I consider this for a moment. I guess it's true, in a way. I went out on a Saturday. I got the bus without worrying the whole way. I clench my hands slightly less when I'm with her. He's right, I've been way more sociable recently. Hell, I left my house on a Saturday afternoon. And went to town. As in, town where people from school go to. I've been bunking off classes, speaking and even texting with a friend that didn't exist in my life a couple of months ago. It's weird how meeting one person can impact your life so drastically without you even realising.

"If you can beat up a girl for Whisper, you can go to a party for her," Prince says with a chuckle.

"I didn't beat up Laura, I just pushed her," I sigh, but there's a shadow of a laugh in my voice.

"Tomato, tomahtoh," Prince waves his hand.

"I don't know," I tell him with a groan. "Parties really aren't my thing…"

"Okay, well think about it at least," he settles. "It would be the perfect setting for seducing your lady…"

I nod, with no intention of actually trying to seduce anybody.

"Promise?" He bats his eyelashes at me theatrically. "Cross your heart and hope to die?" he makes a cross gesture over his chest and gets down on his knees.

I laugh. "Yeah, yeah. Stop. I told you, I'll think about it."

He grins. "You're almost becoming fun, Cooper Nelson."

"Who'd have thought we'd see the day?" I reply.

I lay in bed, tossing and turning, thinking about what Prince had said.

Am I ready to go to a party? No. But the fact that he would even ask me to go, knowing that I would consider it (even if only for a second) shows a difference. I would have laughed him out of the room six months ago if he invited me to a party. Now I can at least picture myself on the way there, if not actually at the event itself.

I turn over again trying to get comfortable, careful not to nudge Max awake. He's curled up at the end of my bed, which he does from time to time. I like it, it keeps my feet warm. Obviously, I'm not going to the party. So there's no point even thinking about that conversation anymore.

But the other consideration… surprising her at her window? That is, somehow, the less daunting option to me. If I went at night, I probably wouldn't bump into anybody I knew. I know where her house is, and it isn't far. I know her mum won't be home and I could probably make it to her window without waking her stepdad up. I didn't get to see her bedroom, but I know it was the one at the front of the house because she had fairy lights strung around the window frame and had a huge W sticker on the glass and beneath it, I could see she had a record album propped up - Nirvana. Predictable, cliché, and so very Whisper.

So, I would get to see her room, I would get to surprise her, and when I think of how happy she was when I surprised her with the exhibition tickets, I find myself thinking that it's probably, as far as Prince's ideas go, not a bad one.

Next week. I'll do it. And I will get flowers, because Prince is right. Girls love that crap.

***

On Monday, Whisper is in a strange mood again. Quieter than usual. I know better than to ask her what's wrong, so I just keep her silent company in class, passing her notes with doodles that I hope will make her laugh. The best I get is a small smile.

At lunch we take our trays and sit down opposite each other in the canteen, sitting and eating in silence. I try to take my anxiety medication discreetly, but she isn't paying me the slightest bit of attention, moving a piece of chicken from one side of her plate to the other with her fork. I'm not sure what to say, it's clear she doesn't want to talk, and I feel uncomfortable in situations like this, unsure of how to maneuver them. My best bet is to just not say anything and be here to listen if she needs it. *Clench, unclench.* Was it something I did?

I pick at my plate and then notice that she's glaring at something behind me. I turn around and see Laura and two of her friends. They're whispering theatrically, hands over their mouths and staring at Whisper. They burst into peals of laughter, cackling nastily. Laura's eyes are still fixed on Whisper, like a lion daring another to pounce first.

Whisper's knuckles are white as she grips her fork and she's grinding her teeth, her jaw tightening.

"Ignore them," I tell her quietly. "They're trying to get a reaction out of you."

She says nothing, her eyes still fixed on staring Laura down.

"We can go and eat outside?" I try again.

129

"I'm not hungry anymore actually," she replies, standing up with her tray. I watch as she walks around the table towards Laura. I can see this going badly very quickly, so I stand up and move across the room to try and prevent a scene. Laura's table has gone silent, the three girls watching Whisper with morbid interest, Laura smirking at her as she approaches. She opens her mouth to say something, but we never find out what she was going to say.

Whisper tips her entire tray of food and drink all over Laura's lap, covering her in chicken korma curry and orange juice. A repulsive combination, to be sure.

My chest tightens and I suck in a breath of shock, and then instincts take over and I start trying to make my way over.

Unfortunately, so has everybody else in the canteen, who have now circled around to watch the show, chanting "fight, fight, fight" at them. Phones are whipped out and videos are being taken. Laura shoots out of her seat screaming at Whisper, her arms flapping around wildly. Her friends back away awkwardly and melt into the audience.

Now it's Whisper who's smirking.

"You're a fucking bitch!" Laura shrieks, a glob of korma sauce dripping down her cheek comically.

"I could say the same about you. I'm sure most of the year would agree with me," Whisper retorts, folding her arms and lifting her chin slightly. At that, a few of the crowd laugh.

Laura is now furious, her nostrils flaring and her eyes bulging. "You're just a fucking jealous tramp. You're a skanky, easy sket and everybody knows it," Laura shouts.

It all happens very quickly. Whisper lunges. She grabs Laura's hair and the crowd all gasp and step back, phones being held up as I continue trying to push my way through everyone.

Laura growls, swinging wildly and eventually clocking contact with Whisper, slapping her around the face with a startling loud crack. Whisper's hand loosens and Laura's long dark hair flies free, but so does Whisper's foot which comes up and kicks her onto the ground. Next thing I know, Whisper is on top of Laura, punching her repeatedly whilst Laura is viciously scratching at Whisper's face.

"Someone do something!" someone in the crowd is shouting, the chants to fight now dead as horror creeps over the group.

"Stop her! Get her off!"

"Hit her back, Laura. Hit her back!"

"Someone, get a teacher,"

"What a psycho."

Finally, I push my way through to the makeshift arena and get behind Whisper, wrapping my arms around her middle and trying to heave her off.

"Get off me!" she screams, clinging onto Laura's arms to stop her getting clawed.

"Someone, help!" I grunt over my shoulder.

A boy from the rugby team pushes through and the two of us lift Whisper off Laura, pulling her away as she kicks and screams, blood around her eyes where she's been scratched. Laura is shaking on the floor, her friends pulling her up and leading her away by her wrists. Her right eye is swollen.

"You're a fucking bitch!" she screams, the crowd finally parting as Laura's friends pull her into the canteen toilets.

The rugby boy lets go of Whisper's right side and I loosen my grip at her left.

I nod him thanks and he says, "No worries," before joining the rest of the rugby team at another table, everybody now eagerly discussing the fight and gossiping.

Whisper is panting and making strange whimpering noises, her fists still clenched.

"Whisper Collinden, office, now." A voice bellows across the hall. It's Mr Gray, his voice stern and his hands on his hips. A teacher must have seen the fight and been unable to get through the spectators, running to him instead.

Whisper inhales sharply, her lips a thin line as she storms after him.

"When Miss Harris deigns to leave the sanctum of the ladies' room, send her to my office as well," he says to nobody in particular before whipping around, Whisper trailing after him miserably.

I sit down at the nearest table and realise for the first time that my hands are trembling.

CHAPTER 9

THE WINDOW

My phone buzzes when I'm on the bus home.

- I got suspended for the rest of the week. Laura, too. We had to sit there and get told off by Mr Gray together, covered in food and all scratched up.

- Damn. Are you okay now? I ask.

- I guess, but my mum is furious! I'm grounded until I'm back at school and I got like a two hour lecture. It was about time someone showed that girl she can't just run her mouth all the time.

- She definitely didn't expect it. I reply with an orange juice emoji and a laughing face.

- Ha. Wish I had a picture of her face. Korma on her lashes!

- You're okay though, right? She said some mean stuff, don't take it to heart.

- I don't. I know what everyone thinks of me and that rumours followed me from my last school. As long as you don't believe them, it's cool.

- I don't believe them. I reply.

She sends me a heart emoji and I send one back. Conversation over. I sigh as I put my phone down. This is going to really drag the week on - I've gotten used to having a friend at school to hang out with. I'm going to go back to being the incredible invisible Cooper until she returns.

I'm just lounging on my bed reading my most recent graphic novel purchase, when my phone vibrates.

- No better time to cheer her up with a midnight window tap than now, my friend!

My mouth tilts in a half smile.

- How do you even know about that?

His reply is fast. **- News of fights always travel fast, especially catfights. Videos all over Facebook! She throws a mean right hook.**

I shake my head, glad I don't have the pressures of social media. I feel even worse for Whisper that the fight videos are circling the social sphere. I doubt she's proud of her actions.

Even imagining a video of me being shared online makes my stomach curl up into itself, like there's a wave inside and it's thrashing against my inner guts. I don't understand how other kids deal with this kind of pressure, this constant judgement from everyone all the time. Posting about their day for everyone to make assumptions about their life... I just hate it. Prince only has Facebook for the events part to keep up to date with local parties, which I guess I understand. But it's definitely not for me. Nope. The thing with social media is you have to be social, something I am certainly not.

- **Will you report the video? Get it taken down?** I text him.

- **Already done it, my friend. The Prince is always one step ahead ;)**

I switch my phone to silent and lay back, my book beside me and forgotten. Maybe Prince is right. Maybe I should surprise her. It would be the most exciting thing I've dared to do since 2001. (I'm half-joking.)

I don't have the flowers I had planned on getting her, but she must be in such a shitty mood that just me turning up to hang out would probably cheer her up. I'll tell her the intention to flourish flowers in her face was there. Or maybe it's better to act like it was a spur of the moment and impulsive act of kindness in response to her situation? I didn't think, I just found myself running to her house? I'll figure it out later.

I'm about to shut my eyes when I suddenly pick my phone back up and text Prince.

- **Okay, I'll go to hers tonight.**

There, now I can't pussy out or I'll never hear the end of it from him.

- **I want a full recap in the morning. At ease, soldier!**

I grin and set my phone to wake me at 1am, lying my head down onto my pillow for some sleep before my evening escapades begin. Who even am I? I think I'm feeling anxiety creeping up within me, but the sensation is different. A different sort of adrenaline rushing through me, a different sort of thrashing in my stomach. I realise it's excitement -

such a foreign sensation that I almost mistook it for panic. I smile and close my eyes.

I jolt awake at the sound of my alarm and hastily switch it off before it wakes my family. I blink a few times in the darkness, my duvet's so heavy and warm. Why did I think this was going to be a good idea? I'm so tired and I know that as soon as I step out of this bed it's going to be freezing.

I imagine Prince's face when I tell him I baulked, incredulous at first and then grinning wickedly as he rips into me for being the world's lousiest drop-out. Goddamnit. I have to do this.

I get out of bed and (surprise, surprise) it's bloody baltic. I layer up, not really thinking about what I'm going to wear for once. It's not like anybody is going to see. One jumper, one hoodie and a puffer jacket later and I'm feeling ready for this ridiculous excursion. I put my hood up to keep my head warm and slowly start to sneak down the stairs towards the front door.

"Erm, excuuuse me. Where are you going?" A slurred drawl from the living room. Bella is sat on the floor in a horrifying tiny dress, her hair big and messy, an impressive haul of McDonalds laid out in front of her. She's chewing on a chicken nugget and swaying slightly.

"Please, don't tell Mum and Dad," I tell her.

She narrows her eyes and shakes a nugget at me. "I won't if you don't."

"If I don't what?"

"Don't tell anybody you saw me eating this junk food. Everyone thinks I'm on a -" she hiccups, "-diet."

"Okay, I promise." I go over to shake her hand to seal the deal but she bats my hand away and orders me to "get away from her nuggets." Moments later she's slumped over, snoring slightly and clutching a chip. I take my opportunity and carefully open the front door, slowly so as not to make a sound as it shuts behind me.

I grab my bike from around the back of my house where it's locked. If I cycle fast, I can probably get to Whispers in just under half an hour. I pedal away and revel in the freshness of the air and the stillness of the night. The rows and rows of houses pass by me and aside from a couple of cars and one rowdy pub that's just starting to chuck people out, nothing's alive. It's nice. I wonder if this is what it would be like if there was a zombie apocalypse, no people anywhere, total silence and peace. Aside from the killer corpses, obviously.

I've never been out when it's so empty, and it feels so exquisitely peaceful and safe. My hands are loose on the handlebars and I'm grinning.

As Whisper's house comes into view I slow down, hopping off my bike and prop it against the fence that borders her house. I look up. There's a small orange glow coming from her bedroom window. She's still awake! Even better. I can surprise her at the window like she did to me, instead of ringing her to wake her up. I check the driveway and her mum's car isn't there anymore, so she must be on shift. Everything is going to plan.

I stand beside my bike examining the front of the house, trying to work out the best way for me to maneuver this. It's not so high, and the porch roof juts out in front of her bedroom window so if I could just get onto that bit of roofing somehow, I would be able to just sit there until she opened the door.

In the end I creep over to the side of the house where their recycling bins are neatly lined up and wheel it slowly beside the porch. I begin to climb onto one. Every movement I make seems to be deafeningly loud, but I know that it's probably just loud to me. My mouth feels dry and I can hear my pulse thudding in my ears and I'm suddenly scared. What if a neighbour sees and thinks I'm a burglar and calls the police?

I stop, sat on top of the bin, frozen. What the hell am I doing here? This was the dumbest idea I've ever had. I cross my arms and stay squatted on the bin, watching my breath mingle with the cold night air.

I pull out my phone and take a picture of myself at the house and send it to Prince. Will I delete this picture immediately in case Whisper ever finds it and thinks I'm a stalker? Yes.

Will it keep Prince off my back and make him think I went and just couldn't wake her up? Absolutely.

I climb down from the bin and make towards my bike.

I stop and clench my fists. Why do I always get scared and chicken out? I've made it this far, I may as well just climb onto the roof and see if she's awake. If she is, great, I'll tap on the window and mission accomplished. If she's just asleep and left the light on I'll scuttle back home and never mention it to her so long as I live. I nod, affirming my own choice, I turn around, and climb back onto the goddamn bin. I slowly sidestep onto her neighbour's high wooden fence. It creaks and shifts alarmingly under my weight. I hold my breath and for a moment I think I'm going to come crashing down onto the bins and wake up the whole of bloody England, but eventually it steadies itself and I am able to clamber onto her sloping first storey roof. I tiptoe along, keeping crouched low at all the windows until I reach Whisper's. There's only a tiny crack in the curtains, and I close my eye and peer through.

My eyes widen. Whisper is lying on her bed, her eyes open and glazed over as she stares at the ceiling. She is limp like a ragdoll and her skirt is up by her stomach. Jack is stood over her, his trousers down by his ankles as he thrusts and grunts.

I can't be seeing this right. I pull back quickly, my heart thumping violently in my chest. *Clench. Unclench. Clench. Unclench.*

No.

I have to be sure...I look through the gap again, and there it is.

I pull away from the window quickly and a stream of vomit comes up. I'm sick on myself, but I don't care.

I want to do something, but I... I *can't.* My whole body is propelling me away, pushing me to run and run and *run.*

I have to get away from this house.

Right now.

I forget about the bins and being quiet, I leap off the roof and land on the grass with a low thud. My body is on maximum flight mode, adrenalin propelling me forwards as I run off the grass, leap onto my bike and pedal, pedal, pedal. I don't even stop to see if they heard me.

I stink of vomit and tears are streaming down my face. My knuckles are white on the handlebars. This can't be right. This can't be right. This can't be right.

But it is.

And it was.

I saw it.

Another lump climbs it's way forcefully up my throat and I vomit again, still refusing to stop cycling, the vomit flying into the night air and all over my front. My forehead is wet with sweat, my arms and legs shaking, my teeth clattering uncontrollably.

I throw my bike down when I get back to my house and open the front door. Bella has woken up and carried herself (and her food) into her room. I rip my clothes off and jump in the shower. The water is hot but I'm shivering, covered in goosebumps and sick. I wash my hair. I wash every part of myself twice. I feel disgusting. I want to claw my eyes out. I don't know what to do.

I dry off and lay in my bed, trying not to hyperventilate.

What do I do?? Do I tell someone? My mum? The police? Do I tell Whisper I know? This could destroy her family, destroy her life. She looked so dead and empty, as though she had given up fighting back. I think of her eyes, her sparkling blue eyes so vacant and lifeless and I get back up and run to the toilet retching bile. Tears trail down my face and I'm sweating.

"Shut up, you're making me feel sick," a voice calls behind me. Bella is awake again. I don't say anything, I just clutch onto the side of the toilet bowl, my hair slick against my face.

"Ugh, that smell." She heaves and backs away back into her room, the stench of alcohol leaving with her.

Eventually I crawl back into bed but I don't sleep. I can't sleep. I have the worst spinny head I've ever had in my life and I don't know what to do to make it stop. How do I make it stop? Every possible scenario I can think of, every possible way for me to take action, makes me want to curl up into a ball and die.

I do just that. I curl up into a foetal position and rock slowly, counting to a thousand and back down to try and calm myself down.

I can't shut my burning eyes, in case I see that scene again. They sting and I gasp a strange sobbing sound that I can't control.

I will never sleep again.

- How did it go? ;)

I ignore Prince's text, turning my phone off completely, resisting the urge to smash it against the wall. I can't shake the overwhelming urge to hide. I know it's not logical, but it's like I just need to get away from everything, everyone, this goddamn dirty world.

Mum comes into my room to wake me up. "Jesus, what is the smell in here?" she exclaims, wrinkling up her face. I think last night I threw my vomit-covered coat under the bed.

"I can't go to school today, I feel really sick," I mumble from under my duvet.

I feel her sit down beside me and she peels the covers from my face.

"Oh dear, you don't look very well. Bella said she thought you were throwing up last night," she adds. "You must have a tummy bug, you can't go to school like this - it'll spread like wildfire. You stay in bed and I'll bring you up some herbal tea and dry toast, see if you can stomach it," she says, opening my window to air the stench out.

I don't reply, I just shut my eyes tightly, trying to block out the sight of what I saw last night.

I inhale and exhale slowly, counting to three in-between. I wasn't lying, I feel really sick. My stomach has been cramping since last night, as though someone has their fist in it and keeps grabbing and twisting then releasing.

I need to try to stay calm and think this through. I can't stay in my room for the rest of my life. I need to focus. However shitty I feel right now, Whisper must feel ten times worse. I have to help her. I have to stop this.

I get out a notepad and pen and write at the top:
Possible Plans of Action.

"Cooper, we have to go to work now, will you be okay on your own?" Dad calls up from downstairs.

"Yeah," I shout back. My voice sounds croaky and my teeth feel furry from puke.

"Mum left soup out for you in the kitchen!" he shouts.

Minutes later, Mum enters the room and I quickly shove the notebook underneath the duvet cover. She has a small tray with a tea and toast on it, her handbag over her shoulder.

"Right, we're off. We will be back around six, call if you need anything," she tells me, like I'm a baby. She puts a hand on my clammy forehead, frowns, then leaves.

I pull the notebook back out.

Possible Plans of Action.
1. Tell Whisper I know + form plan
2. Tell the police
3. Tell Mum and Dad + let them form plan
4. Tell Prince + form plan
5. Do nothing

Five possible options which I can think of right now. I need to assess them, so I write a Pros & Cons column and start drawing out lines from each point, creating a messy spider-diagram.

Tell Whisper I Know

Pros: She will have someone to talk to about it and I will know how she wants to progress with the situation - it's her life and not mine

Cons: I don't know how the f*ck to have this conversation with her, it will make her uncomfortable that I know this about her, she might hate me forever.

I swallow and burrow down a little further into my bed.

Tell the police

Pros: Jack will go to prison where he belongs

Cons: Rip Whispers family apart, everyone in town will know, I'll have to tell police I was outside the window, Whisper might hate me

So far this one is an even worse idea.

I coincidentally hear sirens in the distance and it makes me feel faint, so I resolutely cross out ~~Tell The Police.~~

Tell Mum & Dad

Pros: They will be able to make me feel better + will know what to do.

143

Cons: They will just call the police and then have to deal with all of the above

I cross out ~~Tell Mum & Dad.~~

I look down my pad at the last two options: Tell Prince or Do Nothing. In hindsight I'm not sure why I even considered telling Prince, and slash that off in my head. Lastly, Do Nothing.

My diagram has narrowed my options down to telling Whisper I know and trying to work with her to get out of the situation, or do nothing.

Can I do nothing? Can I just sit back while Jack takes advantage of her like this?

No.

I can't.

I have to do something, I have to try and help.

I have to tell her I know. I have to help her get through this. I have to end this. I cross out ~~Do Nothing~~, rip the page out of my notebook and scrunch it up, throwing it across the room into my bin. Then I throw the pen across the room too, crossing my arms. I shut my eyes and try to breathe again. My hands are so sore from clenching that it stings to try to loosen my fingers.

I will tell her. I will tell her. I will tell her.

I end up pulling a sicky for the next two days, too weak and terrified to leave my room. On Friday, Mum makes me go back in.

I've avoided Prince, I've spoken to nobody. He tried to visit but Mum sent him away, in case I was contagious. Whisper text asking if I was okay yesterday and it made me want to cry with guilt and shame and horror. That she cares that I'm okay because my anxiety makes me too much of a baby to deal with her, who is actually suffering.

Getting out of my room felt like such an impossibility, but now that I'm on the bus to school I feel slightly better, more… awake.

"Haven't seen you in a while, fella," Marvin says to me.

"Yeah, I've been sick," I reply.

"Hope you're all good now," he chirps back.

I don't say anything. I'm not good, not at all, and I'm still not sure what to do about it.

I don't read on the bus. I just sit there and clench my hands and twist my fingers and try to fight the desire to smash my head against the glass window beside me.

As Marvin slows down to a stop, I realise exactly who it is that I need to speak to.

I go straight to Suzie's office, knocking on her door with a pounding in my chest. As school hasn't officially started yet she opens the door with a confused frown on her face.

"Cooper? Is everything okay?"

I push past her into the office, shutting the door after me.

I sit down in the chair and suddenly start hitting myself in the forehead again and again until she grabs my wrist to restrain me.

"Cooper, Cooper stop! What is going on? What's wrong? What's happened?"

"I need to make the spinny head stop," I gasp breathlessly, desperation to calm my head down taking over me. I feel so weak, my head screaming scenes of Whisper and Jack every chance it gets. It makes me want to black out.

"Okay, okay. Deep breaths, deeeeep breaths. You're safe here. Calm yourself… caaalm…" her voice is soothing and eventually it starts to become louder than the shouting chaos of my thoughts and I feel my heart start to slow down, although my bruised fists are still clenched tightly.

"Now, tell me what happened," she says, sitting down opposite me after letting go of my wrists slowly.

"I think my friend is being abused by her stepdad," I blurt out. I feel two things happen very quickly. The first is a feeling of lightness as I share my discovery with someone else, as the burden is lifted off me into an adult with world experience. The second is a steam train of guilt ramming me in the gut for telling someone Whisper's secret. Jack's secret.

Suzie sinks into her chair, her eyes widening for a moment and then her calm, professional persona taking over her features once more.

"You think, or you know?" she asks firmly.

"I know. I saw it."

She sucks in a breath. "May I ask what kind of abuse we're talking? Emotional, physical…"

"Sexual," I croak.

She blinks. "This is an extremely serious accusation Cooper. I need you to tell me who it is you're talking about. Is she a student here?"

This is quickly getting out of hand. I shouldn't have said anything at all. What if she tells the police, or somehow works out it's Whisper? Sweat is now dripping down my forehead, catching in my eyebrows. My stomach is twisting sharply, my hands clenching and unclenching, leaving little dark dents from my nails in the palms. My mouth is dry.

"I- I don't know if I can say," I choke out, white noise echoing in my ears as panic begins to grip me again.

"You know this is something that we would have to get the police involved with, don't you? Now that you've told me, I will have to log this in our system. This is a very serious crime. I need to know the name of the girl so I can help her."

My eyes widen, the sirens from before ringing through my skull sharply. "But what will happen?" I ask.

"I can't say for certain," Suzie clasps her hands together and shakes her head with a sigh. "They would have to speak to her first."

"Who is they? You and Mr Gray?"

She shakes her head again. "No, Cooper, not Mr Gray. As I said, this is a serious matter and the police would have to deal with it, including speaking with her directly."

I feel the blood drain from my face and go cold. "No! No, I can't. I can't say anything," I stammer, trying to stand but finding I don't have the strength, my legs like jelly.

"She doesn't have to know it was you who told me, we can keep it anonymous," Suzie tries, her voice tinted with desperation.

"No. No! You don't understand. I could ruin her life, she trusts me," I gasp between breaths.

"Breath slowly, Cooper. Slowly."

I try to catch my breath, but it feels like someone is sitting on my chest, my lungs won't fill up quick enough. I place my palms on the desk to try and support me but they're getting sweaty.

Suzie stands and walks around to me, patting my back gently until I can breathe.

In.. out… in… out...

Someone knocks on the door. "Not now, sorry. Come back later," Suzie calls out sharply. She turns back to me. "Her life is already being ruined," she says gently. "You could be saving her."

"I can't, Suzie. I just can't. Not yet. Can I speak to her first? I need to speak to her, I need to know if she wants the police involved."

Suzie runs a hand through her hair, her mouth a thin line of concern. "I can't force you to tell me who she is, and until I have a name there's not much I can do. If you insist on speaking to her then speak to her, but remember - she may be scared to act against him. Against her family. But that doesn't mean it's not the right thing to do. The longer we wait to act, the longer she has to suffer."

I let her words sink in. Whisper might be too scared to do the right thing, to make the right decision. Just like I am now. The impact of the word 'suffer' hits me like a heavy blow.

"I'm a coward," I mutter.

"You're not a coward. This is an extremely distressing situation for anyone to be in, let alone you. Cooper, I'm worried about the strain this will have on your anxiety. Do your parents know what's going on?"

I have to get it together. I have to seem strong, or she'll get in touch with my parents. "Yes," I lie.

"Right. Well look, stay here for as long as you need to feel better," she tells me.

She pulls out her laptop and begins writing something. What is she writing? Who is it to? Is it about me? Is it about Whisper? Is it to the police? Maybe they'll come and try and get me to confess.

Suddenly I feel sick, and every bone in my body is telling me to run. Get up and run.

That's exactly what I do.

I get up and flee to the door.

"Cooper? Cooper are you alright?" Suzie has stood at her desk, her brows knitted together.

"I'm fine, I just.. I just have to go," I stammer as I wrench the door open.

I shut the door behind me and run. I run down the corridor, I run out of the school doors. I run through the playground, down the highstreet and I don't stop until I get home. I burst through the door. Nobody's home, they're all at work. I collapse on my bed and I sob. I scream into my pillow and I thrash in my bed and I sob until my throat is like sandpaper and my face is bloated.

I'm woken up hours later by the squeak of a chair and rub my head groggily. I look around, confused.

It's dark, and Prince is spinning in my chair, reading one of my graphic novels.

"About time," he whistles as I sit up.

I rub the back of my head. I really don't want to speak to him right now. "How long have you been here?" I ask him. My throat is sore.

"Not long. Ten minutes? Your mum let me in. I was gonna wake you up but then I thought I'd finish this," he waves the book at me, "and... whoa. You look like shit, man."

"Yeah, I know," I groan, rubbing my face.

"What's going on?"

I consider telling him, but just for a split second. I want to share this burden, but I can't bring myself to share such a personal, private part of her life with someone else. She doesn't even know I know. And telling Suzie didn't go as planned... I shake my head. "Nothing. I just have a lot of shit on my plate right now. I'm feeling stressed all the damn time."

"Lucky for you, I brought some magic potion that will make that stress disappear," he grins, reaching into his rucksack and pulling out a plastic bottle filled with brown liquid that looks like diarrhea. "Whiskey!" He announces, waving it. The murky stuff sloshes in the bottle, and never has anything looked less appealing.

"Where did you get that?" I frown.

"I got one of the kids from school to buy it for me. Poured it into this bottle to take it home, so my parents wouldn't hear the glass chinking. Smart, huh?" he taps his temple with his pointer finger, wiggling his brows.

"I don't drink," I tell him with a sigh.

"You don't drink yet, *amigo*." He now procures two plastic cups from the depths of his bag. "We can just have a couple here in your room. It's just you and me, hanging out. What's the worst that could happen?"

I squint my eyes at him. Normally I would put my foot down, but I guess he's right. I've never really drunk before, just the odd beer here and there. Whiskey is a whole different ball-game. But I feel like shit, and maybe it will stop my brain from thinking about Whisper and Jack and how goddamn screwed everything is right now. I need to stop thinking about it. I'll try anything to make me stop thinking about it.

I sigh and traipse over to my door to close it.

"No need, my friend. Your parents were heading out when I came in. Caught them in the drive," he says, pouring a generous amount of liquid into the cups.

"Going out?"

He takes a sip from one of the cups and winces. "Some concert or something. They were all dressed up. Your mum was looking fit," he adds unhelpfully.

I wrinkle my nose in disgust. "Bella's still home," I tell him, shutting the door.

He shrugs.

I'm not worried about Bella. I can hear the stomping of her feet as she dances along to something, a discreet buzzing sound telling me she has her headphones in full-blast. She wouldn't care anyway, as long as Mum and Dad don't find out. Which they won't.

"I guess a couple won't hurt," I say, taking a swig. It burns my dry throat and I cough out with a choke. Prince just about dies laughing.

"That is rank," I tell him, my eyes watering.

"Take another sip. It gets better the more you have," he tells me, swirling his plastic cup like some kind of goddamn whiskey connoisseur.

I take another swig and it's just as rank. It's like drinking vinegar.

"I'm gonna go get something to mix it with," I tell him.

"Man, that's no fun. But get coke. Full fat!" He shouts out at me as I walk down the stairs. I hear him turn on the playstation.

I grab a bottle of coke from the fridge and traipse back up the stairs, glugging a generous amount into my whiskey cup. Prince follows suit.

"I thought you were anti-mixing," I say with a raised eyebrow.

"I'm driving tonight," he replies jokingly.

A couple of hours later and we're over halfway done with the bottle, the playstation games become increasingly difficult to focus on.

"I need a pee," I announce, standing. The room sways gently.

"Thanks for sharing," Prince replies, his eyes still fixed on the game and his fingers working quickly as he shoots a couple of zombies. I stumble into the bathroom and pee. Half of it goes onto the floor but I can't be bothered cleaning it. Then I hear the doorbell and a girl's voice and sigh. Bella must have a friend over. Now I have to clean the pee.

I pull some tissue paper off the roll and half heartedly wipe the floor, flushing it down when I'm done.

I come back into my room to find Whisper on my bed, jumping up and down behind Prince shrieking, "kill him, kill him now! Aw man, you missed it! That was an easy one."

"Easy for you to say. You try it, if it's so bloody easy," he says, passing her the controller.

I stay rooted to the door frame, blinking as though she's a mirage, a wave of dread consuming me.

"Hey, Cooper," she says over her shoulder, picking out a new female avatar for her turn on the game.

"You okay man? I invited Whisper on Facebook, thought it would be cool for us all to hang out again," Prince says. His sentence trails off as he watches me, frowning in concern.

"I'll be right back," I croak, heading back into the bathroom.

Whisper is here. In my house. And she doesn't know that I know. And Prince doesn't know what I know.

I'm panting heavily, clutching onto the sides of the sink and looking at myself in the mirror. I'm a greyish yellow hue, my skin breaking out in clammy sweat and my eyes dilated.

What am I going to do?

I throw up all over the sink.

I wipe my face with a towel and clear the sink. It stinks of whisky. I take a deep breath, clench my hands to collect myself and go back into my room.

Whisper is swigging straight from the bottle, the game abandoned on the Pause screen. "Whoa, were you being sick?" Whisper asks, frowning.

I nod groggily.

"Cooper doesn't drink much," Prince defends me. "Here, have some of this," he passes me another bottle.

I look at him questioningly. "Water," he tells me, rolling his eyes.

"Down that bottle of water, get some food in you and then you'll be good to carry on drinking," Whisper announces, standing up.

"Carry on drinking?" I frown.

"I'll go make you some toast," she offers, leaving the room.

"I'm not carrying on drinking," I tell Prince as soon as she is out of earshot.

He rubs the back of his head with his hand. "Yeah... see the thing is, I may have told Whisper about the party tonight. And...she kind of wants to go."

"You what? I told you I didn't want to go to that goddamn party." I hiss at him. I forgot about it until now. Of course, now it makes sense. Why else would Prince bring whiskey to mine?

"Technically you didn't say you wouldn't go. You actually said you would think about it," Prince argues, but he's shrunk back a little in his seat. "Look, you don't have to come," he says, his hands in the air. "But we would like you to. And if you do decide to come, you don't have to drink! You can stop drinking right now," he tries desperately.

"Stop drinking right now?" Whisper reappears at the door, a plate with six slices of buttered toast in her hand. "Why would he do that?" She grins at me, dropping the plate on my desk and biting into a slice. She closes her eyes. "Mmmmm. Nothing better than warm, buttered toast," she smiles.

"So... are you coming?" Prince asks me, his hands together.

"What do you mean is he coming? Of course he's coming. Right, Cooper? Because I won't know anybody if you don't come."

"You'll know Prince," I argue weakly.

"Yeah, but Prince will be off with his friends from school. I thought you would come and hang out with me?" She pouts her lips and bats her lashes at me.

I look at Prince who is doing the same.

I feel cornered.

I feel my heart hammering in my chest. I can't go to a party tonight. I can't spend time with Whisper and hide what I know. But I can't say no and let them down.I can't stay home alone thinking about what I know if they go without me. *Clench. Unclench.*

"Fine," I say at last, reaching for some toast in the hopes it will make me feel less sick. Am I sick from the alcohol or from my anxiety? I can't tell anymore, they both feel so similar.

The toast doesn't help at all.

Whisper has disappeared to go and get ready and I can hear her speaking with Bella outside in the hallway. When I peer around the door, I see she's in Bella's room, and Bella is wielding a hairbrush, a selection of makeup sets spread around them like she's about to choose the best weapon to go to war with.

She'll be in there forever.

I finish the rest of the toast, offering the last slice to Prince.

"Eating's cheating," he tells me, blowing out a puff of smoke. I eat it absentmindedly, trying not to worry about everything that could go wrong tonight, about everything that could happen at this party. This goddamn party. *Clench. Unclench.*

CHAPTER 10

A PARTY

When Whisper finally emerges from Bella's lair, my mouth falls slack. Bella has curled her hair and created a strange half-up plaited situation, her black hair pinned by a gold star clip. Her eye makeup is bold and dark, her cheeks rosy and pink with matching lips. She's wearing a dress I recognise from Bella's wardrobe, a simple and teasingly short black slip. Any question of letting her go without me seems to fly out of the window. Have more men tried to do to her what Jack did? There's no way I'm letting her out of my sight tonight.

She throws her leather jacket over the top and puts on her scruffy military boots, lacing them up. "Well? We going or what?"

Prince blinks and hands me the bottle of whiskey.

I turn up my nose, my eyes still on Whisper. "Get that away from me," I tell him, gagging a little.

He laughs. "We'll find you something else to drink," he promises, putting his own coat on.

"Whisper... you look really, really great," I tell her in a low voice, so Prince doesn't hear.

"Really? You think so? I told Bella I'd bring the dress back tomorrow, it's nice isn't it?"

I nod mutely. Obviously it looks ten times better on her than it ever would on Bella, in my entirely biased opinion.

"She's really cool," Whisper tells me enthusiastically. "She made me look like this, I haven't looked this nice ever before," she says, patting the dress down and checking herself in the mirror self consciously.

"You always look great," I tell her. She smiles and looks away as though she's embarrassed. After what I saw with Jack, I don't know how she can ever smile. How long has she been hiding behind them?

"Let's go!" Prince bellows at us from down the stairs. Whisper bites her lip and then goes after Prince. I trail behind.

"Hey, if you don't want the whiskey you can have this," Whisper says, pulling a bottle of pink wine from her handbag. "I brought it for myself but I'm happy to keep drinking the whiskey if you want it? Swapsies?"

I unscrew the top and sniff it. It smells sweet like calpol. I take an experimental sip and it's quite dry and fruity. Much more manageable than the whiskey. I don't want to be sober. I'd rather be sick and drunk than sick and thinking about what I saw, what she's going through, how I'm too much of a coward to help her. I take a determined swig.

"It's not as strong, either," she whispers to me. I nod to her in thanks. Prince seems happy with the resolution and instigates a Sip N Pass rule for himself and Whisper with the remaining whiskey bottle.

As we walk towards Ben's house, I sip my wine alongside them, the alcohol dulling my anxieties quite nicely.

"So, what's the deal with this guy? Will he mind me turning up?" Whisper asks.

"Nah," Prince replies. "He has this 'any girl is welcome' policy."

"What about Cooper?" She asks.

"Anywhere I go, Cooper is welcome," Prince says decisively. "I've always got his back." He nods at me and I give a small smile.

"Cute. A nice little bromance you guys have going on," Whisper teases.

"Until the very end," Prince declares loudly. "Prince and Cooper. Cooper and Prince!" He's shouting now.

"And Whisper!" Whisper adds.

"And Whisper," Prince nods solemnly. "The new third musketeer."

"Thanks for inviting me," she tells him.

"No big deal. Wasn't hard to find you on Facebook, not many Whispers in the world."

I almost feel like I'm enjoying myself as we walk together.

But as we get nearer to Ben's house, swarms of kids begin to appear, laughing in groups, bottles clinking together in bags. I want to fold away, to disappear entirely. I can't explain it, and I don't know why I get like this, but the amount of people around and potential for conversation makes me want to jump into a hole.

I drop back a little behind Whisper and Prince and count my breathing in my head to try and calm myself. In.. out.. in.. out..swig.. in .. out.. swig.

Whisper drops back and to my surprise she grabs my hand. She's peering at me curiously and I allow her fingers to entwine around mine even though my hands are probably clammy. She doesn't say anything. Prince turns around and raises an eyebrow but keeps quiet too, a small smirk on his face as the three of us continue our walk, Whisper's hand laced with mine.

I almost forget.

Almost.

And then I think about how small her hand is, and it turns into thinking about how small she is, and that turns into how Jack could overpower her so easily. My stomach twists and I quickly let go of her hand. "Sorry," I mumble brokenly, wiping my hand on my jeans.

As I look down, I notice a fresh, new and jagged red scar on her wrist and I'm back at her window, looking in at a scene I was too afraid to stop. I should have tapped the window, freaked Jack out into stopping. There are a million things I should have done and I did nothing and now she's holding hands with me and I'm looking at fresh new scars knowing why she hurts herself and I'm still doing nothing.

I take a long swig from the wine bottle.

I need to do something. I just need to work out what I can do.

We come up to Ben's house, a huge detached home with a goddamn pool in the garden. As we approach the woods, I can see that the party is actually spilling into Ben's garden, a gap in their hedged wall offering entrance to and from the woods. It's busy. There are a lot of people. I must have stopped walking at some point because Whisper gives my hand a little tug and looks back at me questioningly.

I swallow, my throat dry. I take another swig from the wine bottle. I try to clench my hands and forgot I'm holding Whisper in one of them.

"Ouch!" She glares at me, pulling her hand away.

"Sorry," I stammer. *Clench. Unclench. Clench. Unclench.* I might smash this bottle if I keep going. *Swig.*

"Are you okay?" Prince has turned to me. He knows me so well. He can probably see my chest rising and falling.

There's just so many people. It's so goddamn loud, the music is coming from the woods - a heavy drum and bass track that I can see girls swaying to hazily.

Every step I take that brings me closer to the party feels like more and more like I have weights pulling me down, trying to hold me in place.

I want to run home.

Swig. Swig.

The wine keeps my throat wet enough to breath without sounding raspy and I let the sweetness of it wash over me. I close my eyes for a moment, counting backwards from 10.

"What's he doing?" I hear Whisper say. Her voice sounds like a melodic echo, far away.

"Just leave him. It's a thing he does. He'll be okay in a minute." Prince murmurs.

3...2...1. Swig.

I open my eyes. Everything is still the same, but a tiny bit quieter. I hear Suzie in my head, her lullaby voice telling me to calm. I breathe. I'm okay. There is no danger. There is no danger. I swig. It helps. My brain feels less tightly coiled, as though someone's twisting my temples and everything is loosening slightly. The taste of the fruity wine is mingling with the taste of stale vomit. Everything will be okay.

"You ready to go, man?" Prince asks. Whisper is looking at me with concerned eyes.

Come on, Cooper. Be normal, goddamnit. I nod robotically and they both grin at me, relieved.

Whisper gives my wrist a little tug and I follow, my legs slightly less heavy.

"So what was that? Like a panic attack or something?" she asks.

"I don't know." I brush her off, not wanting to talk about it. Sometimes talking about my anxiety just makes it all resurface.

She doesn't press. We walk in silence, the sound of our drinks being gulped down accompanying the rowdy music in the background.

I take a deep breath. I'm sick of this. Sick of being me. This is my chance to paint myself as a new, fun Cooper. I'm sick of being fragile, afraid, unsociable Cooper. I want to be a guy who takes action, who has friends and goes out and wouldn't have run away when Whisper needed me most.

"Prince, man! You made it!" My thoughts are broken as a boy with black hair and oversized front teeth wobbles over to us, a lopsided grin on his face as he swings an arm around Prince and leans against him like the Tower of Pisa.

"Guys, this is Ben," Prince introduces us. Ben gives us a single-handed salute.

"Hey, Ben. Thanks for letting us come," Whisper says politely. I give him a curt nod because apparently my mouth isn't working.

"No problem, no problem. Any friend of Prince's is a friend of mine," he slurs. "Hey, Mitch, bro! You came!" He stumbles over to greet his next guest and we continue walking towards the woods. Someone's strung Christmas lights around the trees and they're flashing red and green in a way that is excessively overwhelming for my senses. I find myself clenching my fists in time with the flashes and force myself to stop. They look gaudy and the distant buzzing coming from the bulbs as the electricity pumps through the wires reminds me of old motel hotels in horror films.

Someone's set up a wonky ping pong table and a game of beer pong seems to be occurring, which confuses me for a moment as I thought things like this only happened at Frat Houses in American movies. I clearly have a lot to learn.

Whisper is peering around curiously, now the sole proprietor of the whiskey and drinking it quickly. I swig my wine.

"Oh my God, Cooper look," she laughs, pointing. I turn and see Prince being held upside down by three guys, a tube of beer being poured into his mouth as people chant "All hail The Prince". I actually find myself laughing at how ridiculous it all is, ending with Prince being righted and punching his fists in the air, roaring jubilantly.

He stumbles over to us, his hair a mess. "Did you see that? I'm king of the freaking world!" he shouts.

"Pipe down, Prince. You're king of the beer bong at best. And look - another king is about to be throned," Whisper tells him, nodding at the beer pong where another boy is now being held upside down.

Prince just shrugs. "Was good while it lasted."

I chug more wine, look down and realise I've nearly drank the whole bottle.

"You need another drink? Let's go check out the offerings," Prince says, leading us through the groups of people and into Ben's garden.

Of course he has a pool, and it's steaming, a misty fog above it in the darkness, illuminated by lamps which are set up around the edges, so people don't drunkenly fall in.

The wine is sitting in my belly and giving me a comforting buzz, as though everything is just a little bit hazy and a lot less unthreatening. I might even be close to having fun.

There's a glass table at the end of the garden on a patio. Upon it sits a suspicious looking bowl of murky orange coloured liquid and a plethora of bottles - most now empty - that guests have brought as an offering.

"Whisper helps herself to a spoonful of the bowl liquid, pouring it into a plastic cup and giving it a sniff before shrugging and pouring it down her throat with aplomb.

"What is it?" I ask.

"Some kind of punch. Not really sure. It's quite nice," she says, picking at a piece of fruit which is in her cup and flicking it out onto the grass.

She holds the cup out to me and I take the tiniest sip in the world. "Just tastes like dirty orange juice," I tell her.

Prince takes it upon himself to pour us three full cups and we pass by the pool again and head back for the woods, our drink-acquiring mission accomplished. I finish my wine bottle and discard it in a bush. There is a lack of bins around - I checked.

I'm starting to feel quite good again, the gentle buzz of the music rhythmic and everyone's happiness infectious.

"Beer pong, anyone?" a girl calls out.

"I'm in!" Prince shouts back, bounding over to the table. "Oi, Cooper, come over here. We're doing doubles!"

"I'll come support," Whisper says to me, nodding encouragingly towards the table. I've never played before, and feel horrifically self conscious and nervous - but I don't clench my hands or break out into a sweat. I walk over and the two girls on the other side of the table are setting up their cups, filling them with a revolting mixture of prosecco and beer. One is short with dark hair and eyes, her lips full and pouty. The other is the opposite - tall and willowy and blonde. Both are wearing… not very much. I notice them look at Whisper and say something under their breaths which immediately bristles me, but she doesn't seem to notice. Prince is splashing our cups of punch liberally into the beer pong cups, setting them into a triangle shape.

"I've never played before," I say quietly.

"It's really easy, you'll get the hang of it," Whisper says. "You just throw the ping pong ball and try to get it into the one of the cups on the other side of the table. You're not allowed to bat the ball away when it's their turn, but you can blow it away," she explains.

Okay, so it's not rocket science. But I'm still irrationally scared of making a fool of myself. I want so badly for this party to go well, to be the start of New Cooper. I don't want to mess anything up, to taint my first and only party with a negative experience.

I go to take a swig from one of the cups, but Prince stops me, knocking my hand away. "Whoa, whoa! Not yet, we need those full for the game."

"Oh, right. The game. Sorry," I mumble.

I look up, expecting the girls to be laughing at me, but they're still busy assembling their triangle of cups. Relief washes over me.

"Ready when you are," one of them shouts over.

"Born ready," Prince replies with a wink. He takes aim with the ball and misses so badly that it doesn't even touch the table, flying over to the left. A snort of laughter escapes from me and he jabs me in the ribs.

The blonde girl picks it up and throws it back, this time hitting the table in front of our cups.

"Dammit!" she exclaims, stamping her foot.

"Don't worry - it was close," the brunette tells her. "Next time!"

"Cooper, your turn," Prince says, handing me the ping pong ball.

I throw it without much thought and to my total shock it pops straight into a cup. I blink in disbelief.

"Cooper! You are the MAN!" Prince jumps up and down ecstatically as I burst into a huge grin.

"Woooo, Cooper! You sly dog, you didn't say you were an expert!" Whisper laughs, grabbing both my shoulders from behind and giving them a shake.

"Always a dark horse," Prince tells her with a grin.

"I've never played before," I reply honestly.

"Lucky shot," the blonde girl opposite heckles, plucking the dripping ball out of the cup and downing the contents, putting the cup to the side.

I suddenly notice Whisper is gone, and miss my next shot. I look around worriedly before spotting her at the drinks table by herself and I stop worrying and turn back to the game. The brunette girl manages to get one into our cup despite Prince desperately trying to blow it away as it rolled teasingly around the rim. He succeeded to an extent - blowing it into another of our cups. He downed it the contents with a grimace, evening out the scoreboard.

165

Half an hour into the game and we're winning. I've scored three more points and downed two drinks myself. We've amassed a bit of a crowd, which would usually make me feel like throwing up but right now I'm having too much fun to think about who's watching. I'm sure the drink is helping keep my nerves at bay - I feel the happiest I've felt in a while.

The game ends with us crowned Beer Pong Champions - the girls finishing with only two of our cups left over. I jump up and down with Prince who slaps me on the back, pulling Whisper into a three-way hug, all of us manically cheering with our arms around each other.

The girls concede and our positions are replaced by four new players, me riding on an electric high, fuelled by booze and glory.

"A celebration calls for more drink!" Prince announces, producing a water bottle filled with punch.

"Where did that come from?" I ask in disbelief.

"I nabbed it while you guys were playing," Whisper replied with a mischievous smile. I can't help but laugh.

The three of us find some seats by the poolside and share the bottle between us. The taste seems to get better the more I drink, and I even find myself swaying a little with the music, a lazy smile on my face. This is the most relaxed I've felt around strangers in... years.

"You want to dance, pretty boy?" Prince asks.

I narrow my eyes at him. "Don't push your luck."

"You don't dance?" Whisper asks.

"In public? I'd rather die," I respond. She throws her head back and laughs, the sound rippling through me like a current.

"To be fair, mate, I can't believe you even came tonight," Prince says, taking another drink.

"Is it a big thing?" Whisper asks. She's rocking slightly in her seat, I notice. Or maybe I'm the one swaying.

"It's only the first time in the history of ever that Cooper has left his house at the weekend," Prince tells her. "And he never would have come if it wasn't for you."

I open my mouth to argue but then close it. Am I imagining things or is she flushing? A pink has tinged her cheeks and she's staring at the floor, a strand of black hair falling in front of her eyes.

"You know what I think?" Prince stands up suddenly, knocking his lawn chair back behind him. He glances behind him at it, then shrugs and continues. "I think things are getting a little too hot around here…" he slurs.

"What are you talking about?" I ask, although my ears are going red and I'm concentrating on avoiding any sort of eye contact with Whisper.

"You heard me," he says, stumbling over to me. "It's getting a little hot…" he leans down and grabs me. I stand in shock, and ask what he's doing.

"A little hot and it all needs to just… COOL DOWN!" he shouts, throwing me into the pool.

Everything happens very quickly. The cold water submerges me and I suddenly feel much more sober. I've been drinking, I could goddamn drown, I think to myself with a shot of fear. I push up from the ground and as I emerge from the water a huge splash covers me as another body leaps in. Prince has jumped into the pool beside me.

"Prince I'm going to goddamn kill you!" I splutter as I emerge from the water. Luckily, it's heated, and I've warmed up almost instantly with adrenalin. He's laughing hysterically.

"My goddamn phone could have been in my pocket!" I shout at him, splashing a handful of water in his face.

"Hell!" he curses, pulling his own phone from his pocket. It drips sadly and now it's my turn to burst out laughing.

"That's karma!" Whisper shouts over to us. She's snapping pictures on her own phone, a huge grin on her face. Prince plays up for the photos, pulling a distressed grimace at his soaked phone, his eyes clenched shut and mouth turned so far downwards it's comical. I'm laughing too hard to pose as the flash goes off. I had forgotten anybody else was even there.

Suddenly there's a splash behind us and three girls have leapt in with us, screeching with laughter as they encourage everyone else around the pool to join in. Within minutes the pool is half-full with screaming drunk kids, cups of punch sloshing in and mixing with the water.

Ben comes around the hedge and stops dead, his eyes wide.

"Shit, we're gonna get kicked out," Prince mutters. But instead, Ben bursts out laughing and sprints towards us, canon-balling in.

"I guess it's my turn," Whisper says. Before I can blink she's ripped Bella's dress off and jumped in beside us with a scream. She comes back up breaking the surface of the water, her face streaked black with makeup and she's screaming and whooping, her dark hair slick against her head like a little otter.

"Whooop!" I yell, jumping up and down and splashing around manically. I feel crazy, wild, free. Free from anxiety, from self-consciousness, from the constant constrictions of feeling trapped. The whole pool starts screaming and more and more people start running around the hedges to see what's happening, more bodies joining us and a whole crowd gathering at the edges, getting their phones out filming and taking photos.

Suddenly I feel my stomach clench and squirm. No. Not now, no. I feel it starting to heave upwards, starting at my belly and slowly crawling up my throat. I swallow down hot bile and climb out of the pool hastily, dashing into the darkness of the woods. I make it into the trees just in time before I bend over and hurl, hot liquid vomit exploding out of me. I'm shivering now and it's as though someone's opened the floodgates, more and more vomit falling out of my mouth.

I don't hear Whisper approach, but she drapes a jacket over me as I shiver, rubbing my back gently.

I'm on my knees now and she crouches down beside me, a cup of water in her hands which she offers me. I spit out the last bit of spit from my mouth and take the cup greedily, swishing the first gulp around my mouth and spitting it out before drinking the rest. "Thanks," I mumble, collapsing against the trunk.

I look up at her for the first time and see she's still in her bra and panties, goosebumps lining her chest and legs. Her hair lies like strands of string around her face and she's wrapped a zip hoodie around herself, the arms too long and hanging limply by her hands.

"Who's jumper is that?" I ask through shivers, my teeth clumsily clashing together.

"I don't know, I just grabbed it off the floor," she replies with a small smile.

"I'm sorry you have to see me like this," I tell her, looking at the floor. I'm so embarrassed.

"Hey, it's no big deal. It's not a good party if you didn't throw up," she laughs.

"Really? Nobody thinks I'm a sad case who can't handle my drink?"

"No, you're not the first person to be sick tonight and you definitely won't be the last," she says, nodding pointedly at a group of girls nearby who are slumped on the floor in a pile.

I nod, though I'm not convinced. My first party and I cocked it up.

"You're fine Cooper, honestly," she tells me. She lifts my chin with her hand so I'm looking at her and I look into her deep, sad eyes.

"If you didn't smell of vomit I might kiss you right now," she tells me.

My eyes widen. Goddamn vomit! I hate myself right now.

I look down and take in her thighs, realising they are also covered in white lumpy scars that mirror her arms. I take in a little breath of horrified shock and run my hands down them carefully.

"Don't," she says, pulling the hoodie down to try and cover them.

"Whisper, it's okay," I say gently. I can hear my voice slurring, but I can't stop.

Now is the time. It's just us. I'm brave and reckless with alcohol in my veins. Now is the time.

"You don't understand-" she starts, but I cut her off.

"-I do. I do understand. I know why you're doing it," I say. She says nothing, staring hard at the ground, her mouth drawn into a thin line.

"Whisper, I saw you. The other day I came to your house to surprise you after you were suspended, the way you surprised me at my window," I say.

She snaps her head up, her eyes wide and afraid.

"What the fuck?" she snarls at me, jumping back as though I've scalded her. She whips her head around quickly and takes a step back, her hands held up in front of her. "Whatever you think you saw, you're wrong, Cooper. Okay? You're *wrong.*"

My mouth drops open and I watch as she storms away quickly, running into the garden.

I try to stand up and vomit punch again.

CHAPTER 11

COMFORT

Finally my stomach has wretched out everything left inside of me and I stand weakly, swaying slightly and grabbing the tree for support. I have to find Whisper. I stumble towards the garden and find Prince, now out of the pool and drying himself under the heat of the garden lamps, his breath coming out in little puffs of icy air.

"Man, where did you run off to you little scoundrel? Into the woods with Whisper?" he chuckles.

"I was vomiting up the wine," I tell him.

"Ew, gross dude. You okay now?" he asks, rubbing his hands together.

"Fine. Where's Whisper?" I'm looking around, screening the area but can't see her anywhere. Each wet dark-haired head looks the same and I double-take a couple of times but I'm sure - she's not here. My heart is slamming wildly against my chest, panic building. I am an idiot. I can't believe I chose to discuss The Thing with her whilst I was drunk, wet and vomiting.

"She's not around," Prince says, sitting back into a chair.

"I saw her run this way though," I snap, frustration building.

"Dude, chill out. She's not here. She's probably changing back into her dress somewhere. Look, I'll help you search for her," he gets up and stumbles out towards the woods.

I sigh in frustration and keep looking around. I saw her come into the garden, I saw it. So she *must* be in here, dammit. The only place the garden leads to is the house, so she can't have left without passing by me again.

Then I see an upstairs light turn off and something inside me knows she's gone inside the house - who else is defiant enough to go into Ben's house despite his No Entry signs taped up on every door? I hurry over to the back door and look around quickly before slipping inside. The last thing I need is for Ben to kick me out for breaking the rules and entering his house. I take my wet, vomit-y shoes and socks off by the door and creep inside. I can hear people giggling and stumble into three drunk girls in a toilet cubicle, bent over lines of white powder. When they see me they all start and slam the door shut. "Weirdo," I hear one of them say before the others burst out in laughter.

I carry on through the house, photographs of Ben's rich family hung around in wooden frames and football trophies and medals hung proudly for all to admire.

"Hey, are you new?" I turn to face a girl from my school, Izzy. She's swaying a little, holding onto a small tin of gin and tonic.

"No, I've been at your school since year 7," I tell her with a sigh.

"Cooper! That's it. Cooper." She nods her head a dozen times and stumbles, reaching out to the wall.

173

"Jesus," I mutter, stepping forward and looping my arm under her. I don't have time for this. I have to find Whisper.

Izzy giggles and hiccups in my arms as I try to drag her through into the lounge to put her on the sofa.

"You're never at parties," she slurs.

"Well, today's your lucky day," I tell her.

"You're funny," she smiles, her eyes closed.

I dump her on the sofa and just as I'm about to leave the room, I hear her wretch. I let out a string of expletives as I run to the kitchen and rummage through all the cupboards, finally finding a mixing bowl which I thrust under her mouth.

"Did you see Whisper walk through here? Dark hair, piercings?" I ask the vomiting girl.

She shakes her head tearfully and I go back to the toilet where I bang on the door. "Fuck off!" one of the girls from earlier shouts.

"There's a girl being sick on the sofa. Make sure she gets home okay," I instruct them. I hear the door unlock and before it opens I'm back to searching for Whisper, going room by room.

Empty room by empty room.

I'm upstairs peering into bedrooms when I hear a sound from the end of the hallway. I hurry over to the door and press my ear against it.

"Come on, babe. I know you want this."

Silence.

My heart is pounding in my ears, and my hands are trembling at the door frame.

"Don't be like that, come on," the voice groans.

I hear the sound of sloppy kisses and then I hear the one thing I need to hear to push me past the point of fear.

I hear Whisper. "No. Stop," she mumbles.

I burst through the door and charge at them, the boy leaning over her on the bed, his belt undone. I tackle him onto the floor and Whisper screams, scrambling to sit up.

I punch the guy, some kid I don't recognise from PTS. I hit him again and again, splitting his lip and bruising his cheek and eye. My fist slams into his face and blood is pumping through me, anger and alcohol consuming me.

"Stop! Cooper, stop!" Whisper is screaming, pulling at my shoulder. I turn and she's sobbing, the boy beneath me bloodied and my knuckles bleeding.

I scramble up to stand.

The boy does too, backing away, his hands in the air. "I'm sorry, I'm sorry," he's saying.

"She said no," I growl at him, surprising myself with the menace in my voice. I almost sound intimidating. "Come on, Whisper. Let's go," I start to usher her out of the room when I notice a rip in her top, right by her breast. I turn around and punch the guy in the face, just one more time. His nose makes a sickening crunch and he falls to the ground with a whimper.

Then I shut the door after us and leave him in there.

I grab a towel from one of the upstairs bathrooms and wrap her in it. At some point she put her dress back on and she's shivering. She's still crying, shaking so much she can't speak.

I try to soothe her, but I can't, I don't know what to say, how to form words through my anger, so I just rub her shoulders to keep her warm.

I grab another towel for myself - my clothes are still soaking wet, and leave my shoes by the door. They're

175

wrecked now anyway. I take her out through the front door instead of the back, and we walk down the empty driveway, her head hung low as she cries and me holding her, trying to offer her whatever comfort I can.

"Are you taking me back home?" She asks finally, between sobs.

"No. You can come home with me," I tell her firmly. There's no goddamn way I'm letting her go back to her house with Jack after what she's been through tonight.

- Mate, we need to leave. Right now. I text Prince. I know he can't drive, so I get my phone out and call a cab for us.

- What? Where are you?

- Front drive.

Minutes later, Prince jogs out to the front. "Dude, what happened? Whisper, are you okay?" He's frowning and his breath stinks of booze.

"No, man! She's not okay. Some guy was trying it on with her," I growl.

"What? What guy?"

"I don't know! Some fucking PT guy!" I'm shouting now, and Prince is looking at me with wide eyes. His gaze goes down to my knuckles.

"Damn, Cooper. Did you go all Laura on his ass?"

"She said no, man."

"What?"

"Whisper said no. He wasn't listening to her." I'm so emotional my voice starts to break and Prince sets his jaw.

"Man, if I find out who it was, I'll fight him too," he clenches his own fist and I feel a surge of appreciation for his unfaltering loyalty.

"I'm taking her back to mine. You want to come?" I ask him.

"Nah, you guys go. I can catch a ride with someone else back to mine."

The cab pulls up and I wave a hand at the driver.

"Get home safe, man," Prince tells me. "I'm sorry that happened to you tonight, Whisper." He gives her hand a little squeeze but she's still clutching the towel she's wrapped up in.

I nod to him and hold the door open as she shuffles into the back of the taxi.

"What happened to you?" The taxi guy asks, eyeing up the soggy girl in his back seat.

"We fell in a pool," I tell him. We don't mention the fact she's been crying, her eyes red and her face blotchy.

"Well, don't get the bloody seats too wet," he replies as he pulls out of Ben's driveway.

I open my front door quietly and Whisper follows me into the kitchen. Bella is at the fridge and jumps out of her skin when she turns around.

"Shit! You scared the crap out of me," she hisses. Then she frowns. "What the hell happened to you?" I glance at my reflection in the cabinet and see my face is covered in flecks of blood. I'm still soaking wet and barefoot. My knuckles are basically black. Pair that with Whisper who's wrapped in a towel with makeup down her face and wet hair and we make for a pretty pathetic sight.

"I got into a fight," I mumble, opening the freezer and putting a bag of peas on my knuckles.

"Whisper, there's a downstairs shower through there, you can wash and I'll find you something to wear," I tell her. She pads into the bathroom silently and I feel Bella's eyes burning into the side of my head.

"What the hell happened?" She's frowning at me and sits down at the table beside me.

"Cooper?" She puts a hand on mine and I wince.

"I just got into a fight," I tell her.

"A sexual fight in a shower?" she jokes, her mouth tilting upwards.

"No, I got pushed into the pool by Prince. That's why we're wet. Then afterwards I got into the fight," I say.

"Who with?"

I shrug. "I dunno, some PTS kid."

"Why did you fight him?"

"He was... I was protecting Whisper," I say eventually. Bella bites her lip and breathes out slowly but doesn't say anything. Eventually she gets up.

"Bella," I say. She turns. "Don't tell Mum and Dad?"

She nods. Then before she leaves, she says to me, "Hey, good for you, little brother. I hope that creep came out worse."

I smile at her. "He did." She nods and goes to bed.

I creep up to my room and take out a jumper and some jogging bottoms that will swamp Whisper but it's the best I can offer, and leave them folded up outside the bathroom for her. Then I go up to use the upstairs shower.

I shower quickly, letting the hot burst warm me up and then dry myself off in a hurry. I walk into my bedroom and find Whisper already in my bed, curled up in my duvet.

I climb in next to her and this time it's completely different from the last. I'm not nervous about sharing a bed with her, just concerned. I want her to be okay. I want her to know it wasn't her fault what happened tonight, and it's not her fault what's happening with Jack. I'm definitely not thinking about my penis. If anything, I've never been more ashamed of it's ownership.

I put my arms around her and don't say anything and I feel a wet dribble as she silently cries onto my arm but I let her because I know that in that moment it's what she needs.

Sometimes we need comfort, not solutions.

I let her cry on me until she falls asleep, and then I let the dull aching pound in my knuckles send me to sleep, too.

***

I wake up and find Whisper is already awake, her eyes open and glazed as she stares up at my ceiling. I lay on my back beside her, two matches in a matchbox, and stare up with her.

"Are you okay?" I ask eventually.

She says nothing.

"Sorry. Of course you're not okay."

Still nothing. I swallow. *Clench, unclench.* Don't sweat. Don't sweat. Don't sweat. My hands are clammy.

"I never say no," she whispers, so quietly I almost didn't hear. Her voice is choked. "I never say no and I said it and he didn't care," her eyes start to well up and I hug her tightly.

"He was an asshole. I'm proud of you for saying no," I tell her.

179

She pushes me away sharply. "He thought he had the right. Everyone thinks they have the right with me. And you know what the worst bit is? I bring it on myself. I've said yes so many times that now people think I'm easy, that they can do what they want with me and it won't matter," she spits.

"I thought it was all just rumours?" I ask, thinking back to when I pushed Laura. A horrible shame starts to creep up my neck that I hadn't really considered any of it was true.

"Half of it is, but I let them believe it's all true. That's even worse than it actually being true," she chokes.

"They're wrong, they're all wrong," I plead with her. Why can't she see that they're the monsters, not her? That she's done nothing wrong? She breaks down in fresh sobs and I pat her awkwardly on the back, too afraid to do anything more affectionate in case it triggers something for her. She suddenly looks like she is made of porcelain, a hairline crack decorating her surface, and I'm deathly afraid of shattering her.

"What do you want me to do?" I ask her quietly. "I'll fight them all. I'll fight Jack," I tell her desperately. I just want to make everything okay.

She wipes her tears away, her skin red and blotchy.

"I don't know what I can do," she says, her voice breaking. She sounds so hopeless, so lost.

"You didn't say yes to Jack… did you?" I hate myself for asking, but I have to know.

She stares at me in horror. "Jesus, Cooper. Jesus, no. I just… I let it happen. Again, and again. It's over faster if I don't fight back. When I fight back, he gets angry." Her voice trails off and she sounds tiny.

"I'm sorry. How long has this been happening?" As soon as I ask, I wish I hadn't.

"Years." Her voice is almost so quiet I missed it. But I didn't.

I suck in a breath. "We'll make a plan. I promise. We'll work it out," I tell her.

She nods, biting her lip.

"Does your mum know?"

She shakes her head. "No. She knows I'm sad, but she doesn't know why. She just leaves brochures about teenage depression lying around the house, hoping I'll read one and magically be fixed. Oh, God. What are we going to do about your mum?" she asks, her brows creased in worry.

"Don't worry. We'll tell her I was being sick and you were taking care of me last night. That I slept on the floor," I tell her. "Okay?"

She chews her thumbnail and finally nods.

"How can your mum not realise?" I say, more to myself than to Whisper.

"He's so nice around the house. You saw him at dinner. It's like two different people. She wouldn't believe me. She'd choose him over me, and throw me out." She's crying again now and I hug her tightly until she stops and dries her eyes on her sleeve.

"Cooper," she says, her voice like a small child's as I start to get out of bed. "Thank you."

Those two words broke my goddamn heart.

I bring her downstairs and she hangs behind me like a broken doll.

"Cooper!" My mum can't even keep the shock out of her voice as Whisper and I walk into the kitchen together. My dad puts his newspaper down and peers over his glasses with wide eyes, his eyebrows raised. Bella takes her headphones out.

"We went to a party with Prince last night. I drank too much… Whisper made sure I got back okay. I slept on the floor," I add quickly.

My mum has frozen on the spot, a plate in her hands, but slowly colour returns. "Oh. Oh. The floor, yes." She sets the plate down. "Well, I didn't know you were going to a party." She says the word like she's saying 'orgy.'

"It was a last minute thing," I mumble.

"Good for you! You never go to parties," my dad starts, but Mum shoots him a deadly glare and he coughs awkwardly before picking his paper back up.

"Well whose party was it? Why didn't I know about it? Since when do you go to parties, anyway? Why were you being sick? What were you drinking?" she interrogates me, her voice now shrill.

"It was one of Prince's friends," I start.

"He got the booze from me, Mum," Bella jumps in. We all turn to stare at her incredulously.

"From *you*?" Mum staggers back with her hand on her chest as though she's about to collapse.

"I only gave him a couple of beers, I thought it was more responsible to supply him with a couple of cans than let him arrive and end up on someone else's spirits… I guess he's just a huge lightweight," she says. She looks over at me and I make a mental note to never be an asshole to her again.

"Well, I think that's sensible enough," my dad says. "We were all sixteen once."

"Right!" says Mum, in a voice which insinuates nothing is right at all. "Well, I'm really not happy with either of you. We will be discussing this later," she promises sternly. Then she turns to Whisper and her voice softens. "Whisper, dear. Thank you so much for taking care of Cooper. What a wonderful friend you are." I wince at the way she emphasises the word 'friend,' but Whisper doesn't seem to have noticed.

"No problem, Mrs Nelson," she says. Her throat is hoarse. I wonder if they can tell that she's been crying, that her eyes are puffy and her usual spirit damaged.

"Let me drive you home," Bella offers, setting her headphones down on the table.

Mum blinks at her in surprise. Dad looks at her like she's grown a second head.

"You're going to drive Cooper's friend home?" Mum repeats slowly.

Bella rolls her eyes. "I'm not an ass all the time. Besides, I lent her my dress. We're basically best friends." She winks at Whisper who smiles shyly and then gets up to put her coat on, grabbing her car keys from the side drawer.

"Is he home?" I ask her, my voice a low whisper.

She gives me the tiniest shake of her head. "At work."

I nod, but I don't want her to go back home. I don't want her to leave my side. I want to protect her.

"Thanks for last night," Whisper mumbles to me, following Bella out the front door.

And I'm left with Mum and Dad to deal with. Great.

I sit at the table zoning in and out while Mum and Dad double-team me.

"Should have text us…"

"Girls in your room…"

"Can't believe you were drinking…"

"So unlike you…"

I sit mutely, nodding when I feel it's appropriate and keeping my head down low, feigning guilt while I think about everything that happened last night.

I knew leaving the house was a bad idea. I knew going to parties was a bad idea. But then, if I hadn't gone, who would have stopped that guy and saved Whisper?

I blink, thinking about how he had jumped back when I entered the room. How her eyes were wide and her hands up as though she were pushing him off her. It doesn't even make me feel anxious. It makes me angry. I have to stop Jack.

"Just go to your room!"

I snap back to attention and meekly say, "sorry," as I shuffle out of the kitchen, Mum stood with her arms folded and Dad back to his paper and coffee.

When I enter my room, I have a text from Prince.

- It was Miles Joshwin you beat up. What happened?

I text back the truth. **- I caught him trying it on with Whisper.**

Okay, half-truth. I don't want to embarrass her, admit he was forcing himself on her.

Prince replies, **- Bold move for someone who isn't your girlfriend….**

I ignore it and sit at my desk, my fingers itching for something to do, something to drown out my thoughts.

I put my headphones on, play The Smiths as loud as I can and start to sketch. I sketch and I draw, and I smudge, and I colour and when I finish my head feels quieter and I'm sat looking at a huge drawing of a shattered window, a cracked moon falling through the panes and stars crumbling around it. My world when I looked through her window. I sit back and inspect it. It's actually pretty good. A few touch ups and it would be one of my best pieces. I set it aside for another day.

My phone vibrates beside me and I glance at it, thinking it's Prince again. It's not, it's Whisper.

- **Please, don't tell anyone what you saw. Last night, and at my house.**

I reply straight away. - **I would never.**

I see three little dots appear as she begins to respond, then they disappear. They reappear, then disappear again, as though she can't make her mind up about what she wants to say. My hands tremble as I hold my phone and I feel hot and afraid for some reason. I get up and pace over to my bed where I sit in the corner, watching my phone with my knees up and my chin resting on them.

Finally, a message. - **It's complicated at home.**

I feel a lump in my throat and let out a breath. - **We'll work something out. You'll get through this.**

I want to say we'll get through this, but no matter how much it's upsetting me, it's about Whisper. It's all about her, about rescuing her and about what she needs. It's really not about me at all.

I sit down and try to read one of my fantasy books to take my mind off her, but then my phone vibrates again.

- **I hate Jack.**

Three words she sends me which I know is her way of letting me know we can fight this. We can fight this, and we can put a stop to it somehow. She's letting me know it's okay.

I just need to come up with a plan.

CHAPTER 12

HOSPITALS

I wake up early and open my notebook, titling my page **Possible Plans of Action 2.0**. Then I sit and stare at it for seven minutes. I push it away from me, frustrated. Why can't I come up with a goddamn plan? Or an idea to make things better? I groan and lean back in my chair. I know who would come up with a great plan, but I don't think Whisper would want me to say anything to him. But what if I told him, and it helped to fix everything? A person I trust...

I chew on my pen lid while I contemplate telling Prince.

No, I can't. I'll try to think of a plan on my own first. It's not fair to Whisper. I can't spill her secrets, her pains.

I watch a couple of detective films that afternoon to try and get inspiration for a plan. It doesn't work. I'm quiet through dinner but Mum thinks I'm sulking from being told off, so she doesn't press for conversation.

Whisper texts me once. All it says is, **- Don't worry about me. I'm staying at Ellies again tonight.**

It's short-term relief.

When I go up to bed is when I start to panic. Thinking about school tomorrow and seeing Whisper. I hope I keep my shit together eventually turns into, what if I don't keep my shit together? I start to clench and unclench, and then the sweat comes. When the sweat came, I started to get stressed that I was already panicking, and the tight chest came. It's almost as though I'm panicking about panicking. I felt like I was drowning, falling down a never-ending pit of fear. It took forty minutes of counting with my eyes shut and clenching and unclenching before I was okay again. Then I was so exhausted from it all that I fell asleep, the sheets damp beneath my back.

"Morning, Marvin," I mumble.

"Morning, young Cooper," he smiles.

I sit on the bus and stare blankly at the pages of my Frankenstein book, searching for an answer to Whisper's problem that doesn't involve being a goddamn snitch. Snitches get stitches.

I think and I think, and I think, and I have a big fat nada by the time the bus rolls into the school parking lot.

As I'm getting off the bus, Marvin stops me. "Hey, Cooper? Get yourself some sleep, son. I could carry my shopping home with the bags under your eyes." He chortles warmly but I can see concern in his eyes.

"Thanks, I'll try," I tell him, rubbing my eyes self-consciously. He's right. I probably look like shit. I can't remember the last time I slept intentionally, without falling asleep accidentally or from sheer exhaustion. My mind's been too busy, the cogs manically smashing against each other and speeding out of control.

"Something going on at home?" he asks gently.

"Not really. Just stuff happening with friends."

"Ah," he nods knowledgeably. "Friends, or girlfriends?" He smiles at me and usually I'd smile back, but my face just can't do it.

I sigh. "I think one of my friends is in trouble, and I don't know how to help them. And it's a secret, so I can't tell anyone."

Marvin clasps his hands together on the steering wheel. It's just us left on the bus now. "Well, you have to weigh up if finding the solution to the problem outweighs the breaking of trust. If your friend's in real bad trouble, I'd say it's worth breaking a promise if there's a hope of helping a pal out. A problem shared is a problem halved, or so they say."

"Yeah, I guess. I'll think about it," I tell him. I don't need to think about it - I know he's right. If I break Whispers trust to tell Prince and he comes up with a solution, it's worth it.

"You do that," he nods and gives me a small smile.

As soon as I step off the bus I'm tackled by Whisper, who grabs me from behind. She's still beautiful, obviously, but she looks worse for wear. Her usually preened hair is sticking out all crazy and her eyes are bloodshot and wide, rimmed with circles that match mine. She drags me to the edge of the parking area without saying anything and I follow.

"Look, I need to tell you something," she says, her voice low.

"Anything," I tell her.

Her eyes soften for a moment, then go back to their fearful state. "I wasn't really honest before, when you asked why we moved here."

I frown, but say nothing.

"The truth is, back at my old place, this happened before. One of my friends caught Jack being..." she drops her voice to a whisper, "inappropriate with me. She was too afraid to get involved but it freaked Jack out, knowing what she had seen. He convinced my mum that I was going off the rails in London and that moving straight away would be best for me. He lied about what I was up to, told her he'd found drugs in my room."

My eyes widen.

"He hadn't," she rolls her eyes. "He planted some stuff in there - serious stuff, not cannabis. My mum freaked and the next week we were here," her eyes are welling up now. "I can't have it happen again, Cooper. I can't move again, with no goodbye or anything. I can't leave you, and Prince. You guys are the only real friends I've had in such a long time. My friends back home weren't nice people, they were just people to kill time with, you know? It was all about looking cool and acting cool and it was so tiring. They didn't understand me like you guys do, and I just really don't want to leave and have to start all over," her lips are trembling now and a tear splashes off her face.

I pull her in for a hug and she softens against me. I don't want her to leave. I can't let that happen, she's making me such a bigger person than I ever thought I could be. And she doesn't want to leave me, either. I have to fight for her.

"We'll work something out. You aren't going anywhere, I promise," I tell her. My voice has more confidence than I feel. It's usually me that needs taken care of, that needs calming down. I've never been in this position before, where I've been needed and can help someone else.

That said, I've been thinking for pretty much 40 hours straight now and still have no premise for a plan. Nothing. Zilch. I envision Jack, sneaking around Whisper's room, going through her private drawers and stashing drugs there to frame her. All this, just to keep her to himself like she's some goddamn possession he owns. It makes my blood boil, and soon I'm so angry I can barely think straight.

When she pulls away, her jumper sleeve rolls up. She pulls it down quickly, but not quick enough.

I saw the fresh cut and she knows I saw it. This one's deeper than the other ones. It's messy and jagged and deep. It needs stitches.

"Whisper, you need to go to a doctor," I hiss at her, trying so hard not to raise my voice and attract unwanted attention to our conversation. "You need to get that fixed. It could get infected."

She shakes her head, her eyes hard. "No, it's fine."

"No, it's not." I tell her, surprised by the sternness in my voice. "Look, you don't have to go to a regular doctor. You can do a walk-in at the hospital. Give them my address as your home. Your mum doesn't ever have to find out." I know that's probably what she's scared of, but I can't help but wonder how much of a blind eye her mum is turning. Surely, she must have seen Whisper's scars.

"How am I meant to get to the hospital?" she asks, as though my suggestion is preposterous.

"Prince can take you, after school."

"No way," she shakes her head violently.

"You don't have to tell him why, just say it's… girl problems?" I try desperately.

The corners of her mouth tilt just the tiniest fraction. "Girl problems?"

"Yeah. He won't ask." We stare each other down for a few moments and finally she sighs in defeat.

"Fine. You win. I'll go after school. But you have to come too."

I smile. Then an announcement rings out. "Cooper Nelson to Suzie Walthom's office please." I frown. "Guess I'd better go see what that's about," I say casually, trying to ignore the fact that my throat has gone dry and my chest feels too small for my body. Whisper nods and heads to her class, giving me a sad smile as she walks away.

I text Prince on the way to Suzie's.

- Need you to drive us to the hospital tonight. Whisper has to go, she didn't say what was up other than girl stuff.

His reply comes when I'm sat outside Suzie's.

- Gross, man. Don't wanna know. But yeah, no problem. I'll swing round when I finish.

I sit outside Suzie's office waiting, my vision blurring slightly as I struggle to breathe. What does she want to see me for? Is it about Whisper? Has she somehow found out? When the door to her office opens I see Mr Gray stood with her by her desk, and they both look at me pityingly. Why is Mr Gray in there? What does he want? This must be serious.

Oh God, maybe he's getting the police involved. I try to stand up but my legs are like jelly and I fall back down.

"Cooper!" Suzie rushes over, placing an arm under mine and heaving me up. "Someone get him a glass of water," she orders, the receptionist hurrying over to the water cooler. Mr Gray is soon by my side, supporting me on the left as the two of them pretty much carry me into her office and lay me down on her squishy sofa. I'm drenched in sweat. Someone places a cup into my hands and then guides it to my mouth where I take little sips at a time, my hands shaking violently.

"Breathe, Cooper. Just like we've spoken about, just breathe…" Suzie's voice is coming from somewhere in the room, but my vision is dotted.

"What's happening? Do we need to call an ambulance?" Mr Gray asks.

"It's a panic attack. Let's ride it out, he has them quite frequently," Suzie explains to him in a hushed tone.

Ride. it. Out.

I'm hyperventilating, clenching and unclenching my fists with vigour. I want to run but my legs feel like they're anchors, unmovable. Ride it out. Breathe. Clench. My hands are aching from how much I've been clenching them recently and every clench sending a sharp sting through my knuckles where they're still split from the party. I clench my teeth and squeeze my eyes shut and don't need to count because Suzie knows what to do and is counting for me.

"Ten…nine…eight..seven.. You're doing great, Cooper, six… five…" my breathing begins to slow down, my chest expanding as my lungs right themselves. After what feels like hours, I open my eyes. They go straight to the clock behind her desk. Twenty minutes. I have sat here sweating and clenching for twenty goddamn minutes.

"Have more water," Mr Gray bends down to my level, a fresh cup in his hands. I take it and slurp it down. The pipes in my throat feel too small for the liquid.

"Cooper, there's no need to panic, you aren't in any trouble," Suzie says gently.

"Then why is Mr Gray here?" I ask between breaths.

He sighs and sits down on the couch beside me, which feels odd and overly relaxed, as though we're at his house or something. "Suzie had to tell me about what you told her in your last meeting, Cooper. Because you understand how serious it is, don't you? And I just wanted to see if I could change your mind about telling me the girl's name." His eyes are kind and concerned, not the eyes that I'm used to seeing, the ones that are usually accompanied by barks of, "you're late, get to class!" and "you're suspended."

"I can't tell you, sir. I just can't," I whimper.

"Look, Cooper. We know you've been spending a lot of time with Whisper recently," Suzie starts, and I feel my chest stop. Time stands still. I try not to snap my head up and react, but internally I catch my breath, my hands instantly cold and clammy.

"It's not Whisper," I blurt out desperately and immediately regret saying anything.

Suzie looks sad. Fuck. She knows. "Okay. Okay, it's not Whisper. But if you don't tell us who it is, we'll have to make guesses and bring people in."

I think I may vomit. I glance over at the bin to calculate distance and Suzie picks up on it. She quickly gets up from her seat and brings the bin beside me. I swallow down a wretch. They can't bring people in. They can't bring Whisper in. She'll know I snitched. And if they ask around, everyone will know her goddamn business. It's too much, and I wretch violently into the bin. It stings. I didn't have breakfast, it's pretty much just the water I've just drank, clear and mingled with bile. Mr Gray hands me a tissue and another cup of water.

"Look," I try desperately, "what if I can convince her to come speak to you herself?"

There's a pause and Suzie looks to Mr Gray as they consider my proposition.

"I don't want you guys interrogating Whisper or any other girls, it will just cause drama and gossip," I babble. Mr Gray frowns. If there's one thing he hates, it's drama. Especially when it's to do with girls.

"I think we could make that work," Suzie begins slowly. "But we will need to be catching up with you frequently about this, until the girl comes to speak to us herself," she adds, looking to Mr Gray who nods. My chest relaxes. I've bought us some time.

I nod. "I'll speak to her, I promise."

"Okay. Well, if you're feeling better you can head off to class."

"Actually, sir, I'm really not feeling good," I say. I can see my hands have gone a strange grey colour and I can feel drips of sweat running down my cheeks.

Mr Gray nods. "Go home today, Cooper. Rest up. But be back tomorrow," he adds sternly.

I stand gratefully and try not to sprint out of that goddamn office.

Luckily Marvin is still sat in the bus outside – I really don't want to have to call Mum for a lift home and play sick again. I hobble over to him sadly. "Marvin? When's your next shift?"

"I got to go to the old people's home in…" he checks his watch, "thirty sweet minutes." He frowns. "What's wrong, kid?"

"I'm sick," I tell him.

"Say no more, hop in. I'll drop you home before I have to go to the coffin-dodgers." He laughs at his own joke.

"Are you sure?" I ask.

"You're damn right I am. Get in, son."

I climb into the bus and sit behind him, even though the bus is empty aside from me. My house is only fifteen minutes away, and Marvin chats the entire time, so I don't have to.

"Get well soon, Cooper," he tips his head at me.

"Thanks, Marvin," I say. And I really mean it.

When I'm in my room I text Whisper.

- Had to go home, I got sick after my meeting with Suzie. But I'll still take you to the hospital. Come over after school.

I never see her reply because I crash out. Being constantly afraid and anxious is goddamn exhausting.

I'm awoken by Prince diving onto my bed with a roar. "Jesus!" I shout. "You scared me out of my goddamn mind." I clutch at my heart as he laughs.

"I'm here to take your fine lady to her destination." He stands and does a theatrical bow, his hand fluttering in front of him.

"She's not here yet," I tell him, rolling my eyes.

"You sure?" He asks, lifting my duvet cover and pretending to check underneath.

"Jesus, have some bloody decorum," I tell him.

He grins and slumps onto my bed. "So, where is she? What's the deal? Is it downstairs problems?"

I throw a pillow at him which he ducks and misses, the pillow thudding against the wall before dropping onto the bed.

"I don't know. And I didn't ask, I'm a gentleman," I reply.

My phone starts to buzz and it's Whisper. I don't really like taking phone calls, but it could be important.

I clear my throat self-consciously. "Yes?"

"Hey, I'm outside. You ready to go?"

"Yes." I hang up without another word.

Prince raises an eyebrow. "Are you a spy or something?"

"Maybe. Let's go," I tell him, throwing my coat on.

He rolls off my bed and we meet Whisper by Prince's piece-of-shit Ford KA which is parked outside.

He opens the door for Whisper, motioning her in with a hand. "Your carriage awaits, m'lady."

She rolls her eyes but grins as she gets in. I climb in the front.

When we arrive at the hospital Prince does two rounds of the car park before huffing in frustration. "I'll drop you two kids off and find somewhere nearby to park. Who knows when a space will free up, and I bet it's bloody extortionate," he tells us, pulling up at the drop-off point. I salute him with one hand and open Whisper's door with the other.

197

"I'm getting the real princess treatment today," she laughs.

"Only what the lady deserves!" Prince shouts from the car. I slam the door in his face.

She links arms with me as we go up to the reception.

"May I help you?" The woman behind the counter peers down at us, her eyes tired and bored.

"Yeah. I think I need...uh.. stitches," Whisper mumbles.

The woman looks up and puts her pen down. "Stitches?"

Whisper glances to the side then sucks in a breath and pulls her sleeve up. She has tried to bandage it but the amount of fresh blood seeping through is terrifying. The woman's eyes widen for a moment before she regains her composure. "Right, yes. Sit down, keep your arm elevated and fill this form in and then wait for your name to be called. Hopefully it won't take too long" she tells us, pointing us towards a very depressing waiting area. I look around as Whisper writes her details down for the receptionist.

It stinks of disinfectant, bleach, and sadness. The fluorescent lighting above is bright and gives everything a sickly yellow tinge, and all on the walls are posters and brochures for leisurely reading.

5 Signs you have depression.

Have you had a flu vaccination yet?

How to deal with aspergers - a family guide

Smoking Kills. Quit today.

It makes me feel sick just being in here.

Whisper sits back down beside me having handed her form in. She cradles her arm absentmindedly. "Pretty bleak in here, huh?"

"My thoughts exactly," I reply.

A text from Prince buzzes in. **- Only parked on the other side of the bloody country. Walking up now.**

"He's on his way," I inform her.

She nods, wringing her hands in her lap. "Hey, thanks for... well, for everything. I don't know what I'd do without you," she says.

I'm about to tell her it's not a problem (like I always do,) when she turns over, takes my face in her two hands, leans in, and kisses me. It isn't like a porno kiss, it's soft and quick and gentle and she tastes of mint and sticky lipstick and I don't even move because I'm so shocked. She pulls back quickly and sits with her back straight, staring at the wall ahead as though nothing just happened. I don't need a mirror to know I'm as red as a goddamn blister. My heart is pounding so hard I think it might rip right out of my chest, smashing through my ribcage. Is my heart even behind my rib cage? I don't know. But if it is, it'll smash through, I'm sure of it.

I'm gripping the sides of my chair and staring straight ahead too, both of us not wanting to look at the other. In her case, probably because she's repulsed and regretting her choice. In my case because there's a very real chance I'll get a stiffy.

Then, the one thing that would kill any boner in the history of boners happens.

Prince walks in.

"Bloody parking in this place is a shitshow," he huffs, slumping down next to me and picking up a brochure for STDs absentmindedly before seeing the cover and hastily throwing it back down. "Hey, why are you so red?" he asks, peering at me.

Naturally, I go redder. I don't dare look at Whisper.

"Just hot. Going to go get a drink," I tell him, heading over to a vending machine and trying to make my walk look casual. I risk a glance back and Whisper is scrolling through her phone, looking as unbothered as anything. Then she looks up and smiles at me. This girl kills me.

I let out a smile of relief because she isn't:

a.   Wanting to throw up following a physical interaction with me and

b.   Acting awkward enough that I will get more uncomfortable.

I need to calm down.

I saunter back, flick my hair and sit down next to Prince.

"Hey, look, this is you," he says, stabbing a picture of an obese man on a brochure that reads, *Obesity costs the NHS £5 billion a year.*

"Shut up," I tell him, crumpling the brochure in his hands.

"Hey, this is you," Whisper says, leaning over with a brochure that says *Dealing With Your Sexuality* on the front, pointing at a cartoon with a speech bubble above it that reads, *What is a Hermaphrodite?*

"Alright, alright, good one," he grins with a roll of his eyes.

We continue playing the This Is You game with as many brochures as we can find for the next hour before Whisper's name is finally called by a nurse who beckons her to follow. She gets up and follows without even looking back.

"She's cool, isn't she? Like, we can hang with her even though she's a girl, you know?" Prince says absent-mindedly, flicking through a copy of House & Home magazine and peering closely at a blonde yummy mummy in an apron.

"Yeah. Yeah, she is," I reply.

She's out just under half an hour later and gives nothing away. "All good now guys. Thanks so much. Prince, remind me to buy you a bottle of something bad for you as thanks," she says. She positions herself between both of us, linking arms with us but I notice she puts her arm through mine a little carefully and I know that her stitches are probably sore.

"Ah, in that case we need to go on these adventures more often," Prince replies with a smirk.

We drop Whisper home and Prince comes back into mine despite not being invited. I don't really mind though. As soon as we're in my room he leans out of the window for a smoke. I want to bring up that he could have smoked at the hospital, walking to the car, in the car, at Whisper's house, basically anywhere other than my bedroom. But I don't, because he sat in a waiting room with me for two hours because I asked him to and didn't even complain.

I tried to get her to come back to my house, but she refused. She said her mum would be home tonight, and then gave me this meaningful look that translated into, nothing bad can happen to me while my mum is home. Still, I hated dropping her home. I hated knowing who we were leaving her with. I hate knowing that even though she's all stitched up now, there may be new scars tomorrow because nothing's really fixed.

I'm busy thinking about all the things I hate when a tennis ball hits me on the head.

"Ouch! Where did this even come from?" I grumble, turning the ball in my hand.

"Where did you just go to, space cadet?" Prince asks. He's smiling but a strange concern flickers behind his eyes.

"I dunno. Just thinking about stuff," I say.

"Ah, stuff. What sort of stuff might that be?"

In this moment I go over the millions of things I want to say, the tiny proportion I'm actually allowed to say, and I sit there in silence for what feels like days contemplating how much to tell him. Marvin was right. A problem shared is a problem halved, and if we can fix this, it'll be worth anything. Even losing her.

I make a snap decision. I may regret it for the rest of my life but I decide I'd rather regret acting then sitting back and letting all this keep happening. Doing nothing is as bad as participating, sometimes.

"Prince, I need to tell you something and you have to swear on your goddamn life not to tell anybody, ever. But I just can't handle this type of shit on my own," I tell him quickly.

"You have my attention," he says slowly, sitting forwards.

"No, you have to swear on your whole family's life first that you won't tell anyone. Swear it?"

He licks his fingers and holds them in the air in some kind of rip-off cub scout salute, closes his eyes and says, "I swear it."

"This is serious," I chide.

"Dude, I know. I'm taking it seriously, I swear. You're freaking me out. What's going on?"

I breathe out slowly. "You know that night I went to Whisper's and climbed up to her window?"

"...yes?"

"I saw something."

"Was she doing naughty things to herself?"

"Shut up man, I just told you this is serious."

"Sorry, sorry," he says hastily, worried I'm not going to tell him after all.

"Her stepdad... he was raping her." The word tastes like poison in my mouth.

Prince stays very still and says nothing for a while, as though frozen in the spot. Finally, he reaches into his pocket, takes out his cigarettes and stands to walk towards the window. "Fuck."

"Yeah. Goddamn right, fuck. And today, at the hospital? She's hurting herself and it's getting worse and we need to stop this, and I don't know what to do," once I start, I can't stop. I tell him what she told me about the drugs being planted and having to move and Prince says nothing, smoking his way through two cigarettes back to back before I'm finished. "I've been going out of my goddamn mind! I don't know what the hell to do, who to go to, I'm totally out of my depth," I confess. It feels like a weight has been lifted off my chest and for a moment I can breathe and get through this. Prince will know what to do. Prince always knows what to do.

He nods slowly but says nothing. For a really long time he says nothing. He grinds his cigarette on the windowsill, closes the window and sits down on the bed beside me. He sits there in silence for ten minutes and then gets up and begins pacing up and down my room, frowning and looking at his feet.

He opens his mouth, then frowns deeper and closes it, his lips drawn in a thin line as he continues to pace and pace and pace.

Eventually he sighs, sits down next to me and says, "This is some next-level Gossip Girl shit."

"I never watched that show," I tell him.

"Look, I gotta sleep on this. Good plans take time. I'll come up with something and speak to you tomorrow. Hang tight," he gets up and puts his coat on. Then, to my surprise, he comes back over and gives me a quick hug. "We'll sort this out, man."

"Thanks," I tell him.

We have to, for Whisper's sake.

CHAPTER 13

THE GREAT PLAN

As usual, I barely slept. I just kept going over different plans of action in my head, each getting more and more ridiculous and unrealistic. At least an hour was spent working out how we could cover up a murder, so we could just get rid of Jack completely and pretend he never existed.

"Cooper, dear? Are you okay?" Mum asks me as I pick at my toast.

I nod, my brain consumed. Will Prince come up with a plan today? Will it be a good one? What am I willing to do for Whisper? How far will we have to go? Will we actually have to kill Jack? What if I have another panic attack during the plan? Could I handle losing Whisper?

Even Bella is frowning at me as she shovels cereal into her mouth.

"Yeah, fine, just got a test I'm trying to go over stuff for in my head," I lie.

Mum seems satisfied with the answer and smiles at me. "Good boy," she tells me. Max lifts his head and looks at her. "Not you, you, silly old boy," she tells him warmly, throwing a bit of my toast crust at him.

As I get up to leave, Bella grabs my jumper from behind. I turn to her.

"Hey, everything's okay, right?"

"Yeah," I tell her. I feel so tired.

"With Whisper, I mean. I feel like… well, when I dropped her home that day, it just felt like something really bad had happened," she says.

I purse my lips and stay quiet.

"Look, you don't need to tell me anything, and her business is her business, but she needs to tell someone if something really bad happened at that party," she tells me, staring at me hard. I swallow. If only you knew Bella, I think sadly, the worst possible thing that could happen is happening in her home.

"Thanks," I tell her, before shutting the door after me.

I sit by my bedroom window like a stressed dog awaiting his master. In history class today, Prince text me, **- I have an idea. Meet me after school. Let's take this bastard down**. I knew he would come through.

As soon as Prince's crapwagon appears at the end of the street I hurdle down the stairs and fling the front door open. He steps out of his car, his trademark half-smile. "Am I genius, or am I a genius?"

"Yeah, yeah. Get inside and spill your plot of grandeur," I say, ushering him into the house. I'm basically dancing on the spot with anticipation. This could be it, the answer to everything. I bet it's obvious, something easy I should have thought of days ago. We're going to make everything better.

"Well? " I ask him as soon as my bedroom door is closed.

"Okay. But you might not like it…" he warns.

I nod, a butterfly hitting against my stomach walls. I knew an easy answer was wishful thinking.

"Right. So we basically need to scare the shit out of him. Make him think we want to go to the police, even if we don't. We need to scare him out of ever doing it again, make him think he's going to be outed to the world as the paedo he is," he explains. He's stood in front of me as though he's a teacher.

"So… we're going to threaten him?" I ask slowly.

"Kind of, I guess. We need to make him think we have something on him, some kind of evidence. And then use it to blackmail him."

"Last time someone found out about them, he upped and left. We can't let him take her and leave again, it'll just happen again somewhere else," I tell him.

He frowns. "That's why we need something that puts us in control. We have to hold something over him," Prince explains.

My stomach knots itself slowly, folding in over my intestines and wrapping around like a worm. "But we don't have evidence, and I don't want to repeat the whole window charade to get any."

Prince pinches the bridge of his nose as though dealing with an imbecile. "We don't need evidence, we just need him to *think* we have evidence," he says slowly.

"Right. Okay. Well that makes things easier," I say. AKA, thank God I don't need to creep over to her house again.

"So what kind of evidence are we talking here? A voice recording? Pictures? Videos? What can we do that will make him think we're telling the truth?"

Prince pouts thoughtfully, taking his usual spot by the window and taking out his cigarettes.

"Yeah... he may know we're calling his bluff…" he rubs his chin and takes a drag of his smoke. Then his eyes light up. "We can take photos of him, candid ones like following him around and stuff. Then he'll know he's been followed and that we've seen something."

He stubs his half-smoked cigarette out in excitement and hurries over to my desk, grabbing a pen and paper. He's scribbling so quickly his writing is almost illegible, but the message is clear.

"Jack,

We know what you've done to your stepdaughter. Don't ever touch her again or we will send the rest of the photos to the police. (Photos of a paedo in the act will be enough to convict, we're pretty sure.) If you leave town with her, the police will know. Kidnapping is criminal, isn't it?

We'll be watching."

I read it twice, then grin. "Brilliant! This is some thriller-movie-shit right here. This is perfect, I'd be so freaked if I found out someone had been following me around in secret."

Prince puffs his chest out. "Yep, well, I am the second smartest in my chemistry class for a reason."

"A fine feat indeed," I reply.

"So stage two: Acquiring said photographs."

I bite my thumbnail. The thought of following Jack around makes me feel sick. "I don't know. I don't know if I can stand to look at him," I admit.

"We'll go together," Prince says. In that moment I love him - probably the most any man can platonically love another man. "Let's find out where he works, that will be the easiest one."

He picks my laptop up from my bed and goes into Google. "What's his second name?"

"Erm… if Whisper's using his name rather than her real dad's then it would be Jack Collinden," I tell him, crossing my fingers.

"Jack Collinden…" Prince repeats, typing it into Google.

A million Jack Collinden's pop up, but then I see his image on Google Images. "There! That's him!" I jab my pointer at the screen. He's smiling at the camera, his perfectly straight white teeth shining and he's wearing a suit with his hair slicked back.

"Slimy son of a bitch," mutters Prince, clicking the picture. It takes us through to a company website called Elysian Tower.

It's some sort of financial advisory company, and it's based in the outskirts of London. Prince whizzes through to the contact section of the site.

"This says their working hours are 9-6, so if we can get there for, say, 5.30pm, we would be sure to catch him leaving work," he says triumphantly.

I rack my brain for a reason that it won't work, a reason it's a terrible idea. I come up with exactly none.

"We'll go tomorrow after school," Prince tells me. "Wear black. We need to look inconspicuous."

"Got it," I tell him.

He goes home and leaves me with my thoughts. I feel strangely calm. I wonder why it is that I can be about to stalk a rapist for illicit photographs and feel totally cool with it, but the thought of walking down my school corridor and saying hello to someone makes me want to vomit. Or why my phone buzzing with an unknown number sends terror down my spine. The mind is a complicated thing, perhaps it's best for me to accept I am the way I am rather than dig around the why's and how's.

I text Whisper before I fall asleep. **- Is your mum home tonight? If not, you want to sneak out and come to mine?**

She replies back straight away. **- Watching a film with her, she's back at work tomorrow. I'll tell her I'm staying at a girlfriends tomorrow and come by?**

I sigh with relief. **- I'll keep the window open.**

As I go to sleep, I begin thinking about our kiss, about how we haven't really spoken since. What did the kiss mean? Did it mean anything at all? Will it happen again tomorrow? Is she lying around thinking about it? (Probably not.)

Suddenly my brain flicks and I find myself thinking about what she could be lying around doing, and it makes me feel a bit sick. I hate Jack. I hate Jack and I want him to pay for what he's doing.

The next day at school is going painfully slowly. Whisper is late in and when she arrives she's avoiding eye contact with me. I can see her eyes are red-rimmed and she shuffles over to her desk and stares blankly at the board. Her sleeves are pulled down covering half of her hands and she's clutching the ends in her palms, holding them in place. I try to make eye contact with her but she won't look over.

I text Prince. **- I can't wait for tonight. Jack needs to meet his swift demise.**

Then I text Whisper. **- Everything ok? Your Mum was home last night, right?**

I watch her take her phone out of her pocket and type out a quick response. **- Yeah. Until she got an emergency call and had to go out for a couple of hours.**

I try to look at her but she's staring at her desk. My pen shakes between my fingers as I fiddle uncontrollably. I feel sick and hollow in my stomach, that she's still living in the same house as that goddamn monster. That we all thought she was safe last night and she wasn't. I'm so goddamn angry. My fists are clenched and I want to smash this goddamn table in half and -

"Cooper? Cooper, did you hear me?"

I start, looking up at the teacher who is frowning at me with her hands on her hips. Sniggers ripple around the class and I feel my cheeks begin to burn.

"Sorry, Miss," I mumble.

"If you were paying any attention at all, you would have heard my question," she sighs, pointing at the sentence she has scrawled onto the whiteboard.

Who is the true monster in Mary Shelley's novel? Dr Frankenstein, or the creature?

I chew my lip, my copy of Frankenstein beneath my hands. I clear my throat. I can feel everyone looking at me. Everyone except Whisper, who is slumped over her book with her chin resting in her palm, staring ahead as though she's on another planet entirely.

"I believe Dr.Frankenstein is the monster, Miss," I reply, my voice steely.

She raises an eyebrow. "Interesting theory, Cooper. Many people could argue Victor Frankenstein was just a lonely, grieving old man. Can you expand?"

I shuffle in my seat slightly. "He's a control freak." I pause as people begin to giggle, then fix my gaze on the teacher and carry on. "He's a control freak and that's why he created something. It wasn't about science, if you ask me. He just wanted to be in control of another life. It doesn't matter what drove him to do it, it was just plain wrong."

I notice Whisper turn around to look at me, her mouth parted open.

"Creature was afraid and just wanted to escape, to hide away. Creature is intelligent, and motivated, and teaches himself how to survive despite everything going against him. Frankenstein made him feel isolated, and alone, and like nobody cared about Creature or his feelings. But I do. I care,"

I know I'm raising my voice now and people are blinking at me in shock, but I can't stop.

"Creature just needed revenge - no, *justice* - for all that Frankenstein had put him through. That's why he killed Clerval, and Elizabeth. It wasn't cold-hearted murder, it was an act of desperation. Wouldn't you do the same, Miss? I know I would. And then Frankenstein gets hypothermia because he is exhausted from devoting his life to terrorizing Creature, and that's what he deserves. That's karma, Miss, and he has nobody to blame but himself. You can't commit your life to ruining someone else's without retribution. That's why Frankenstein dies, because he deserves it. And finally, Creature can have some peace. And Creature blames himself, but shouldn't, because none of it was his fault. None of it."

I stare Whisper in the eye and see that they're watering.

"But you know what, Miss? I think there's a reason we don't know what happens after Creature drifts away to sea. I think that he lives. He goes on to live and to survive because without Frankenstein there to terrorise him he can start fresh. And that's what I think." I stop short, surprised at myself at how long I was speaking for, the whole room now staring at me. I look to Whisper again but she's turned away now, her face covered.

"Well said, Cooper," the teacher says, turning back to the board.

I slump into my seat ignoring the stares and murmurs around me. Particularly, a pair of blue eyes.

When the bell finally rings, I hurry out of my seat and grab Whisper by the arm.

"What was that all about?" she hisses at me.

I ignore her question. I can't handle this anymore. I can't let her spend another moment near Jack, I can't let her keep pretending it's not happening, to keep on hurting herself. She needs help. She needs to wake up and stop blaming herself.

"Whisper, I think you should speak to Suzie about what's going on."

She stares at me as though I've asked her to cut out her own innards and feed them to me.

"You don't have to tell her everything, but at least tell her that you're hurting yourself. It needs to stop," I tell her.

Her eyes drop downwards. "Look, it's really not a big deal,"

"It is a big deal!" I say, frustrated. She blinks up at me.

"You're hurting yourself and it's hurting me. I can't stand it, Whisper. I can't stand seeing what you're doing to yourself all because of Him, and I can't stand not knowing how to help you or what to do. It's goddamn killing me," I tell her, emotion cracking in my voice.

She nods slowly. "I'll think about it."

I can't ask for much more at this stage. But I make a mental note to harass her about it every damn day until something happens.

We're in Prince's crapwagon and he's crawling up to the building that Jack supposedly works at. I'm wearing a black hoodie and beanie. Prince has worn a black cap, jumper and sunglasses, which look ridiculous considering it's already dark out. Luckily, street lights are illuminating the pavement outside.

"Make sure your phone is set to flash turned off," Prince says. "Last thing we need is for him to catch us snapping shots from our car like a couple of perverts."

"He's the only pervert around here," I mutter, but I double check my phone settings anyway, just to be sure.

Prince has turned the music off and we've pulled over on the opposite side of the road, slipped between two other parked cars. The silence in the car is making me jumpy. The building is huge and looks a bit like a prison, with loads of windows and a greeny-yellow lighting illuminating the interior. I watch as people traipse from desk to desk and tap away at their keyboards.

"It's like a proper stakeout," Prince hisses.

"Why are you whispering?" I whisper back.

"I don't know. Just feels right," he replies. Then he leans across to my side and opens the glove compartment, producing a pair of binoculars which he holds up to his face.

I blink at him incredulously and snort with laughter.. "Binoculars? Who do you think you are?"

"I didn't want to miss anything," Prince replies.

"Well, you'll miss him regardless of whether you have the binoculars or not. You haven't seen him in person like I have."

"I can tell what someone looks like from a photograph, you idiot," he responds, bringing down the binoculars down from his face and glaring at me. "Shit!" He suddenly jumps, pulling them back up to his face.

"What?" I spin around to the window and see a woman in a tight skirt suit exiting the building.

"We nearly missed the sexy mama," Prince grins, his binoculars touching the glass of the window.

"You nearly gave me a goddamn heart attack," I tell him, clutching my chest as my heart slows down.

"Shit!" he says again as he brings the binoculars down and grabs my leg. "That's him, isn't it?" he whispers to me.

I look out the window and see Jack, walking towards the car.

"Put the fucking binoculars away, they're drawing attention to us," I hiss, lowering myself in the seat as far as my lanky legs will allow. Prince follows suit. My heart is beating loudly, drumming in my ears as my stomach thrashes with nerves.

"Take the pictures," he prods my arm.

"Oh right, yeah, shit," I fumble to switch my phone to camera mode and hold it up to the window. I zoom in as far as I can and click his face, so the light adjusts, snapping several shots in a row. I catch him walking all the way up to our car and start to freak out. "Crap, let's go. He's going to see us!" I panic.

"No, man. Keep cool. We're good. Look," Prince nods towards Jack who has turned the other way and is heading towards a red Merc that's parked a few cars away from us. I breathe out in relief and quickly zoom in on my camera to get some shots of him getting into his car.

"Quick, let's go, now," I say. "We can get back to their house before him and catch him outside his house, too,"

"Great idea, strong improv," Prince nods, wrenching the gearstick and pulling out of the space hastily. "To Whisper's house we go!" he shouts dramatically, hitting the accelerator as we make our way back towards town.

I turn the radio on and fist bump him, his one hand on the steering wheel. "Boys on a mission!" I laugh.

I feel exhilarated, but also slightly sick with underlying nerves about something going wrong. But for now at least, part one of our plan is complete.

We pull up at Whisper's house and wait - Jack can't be far behind us. The light is on in her bedroom and we can see her walking around, flitting between the open curtains in a dressing gown. I watch with my mouth open and the next time she walks past, she's wearing only a bra and is holding a towel. I gasp and turn around quickly, looking at Prince. "Don't look, man!"

"I can't see past your fat head anyway," he grumbles, sinking back in his seat and folding his arms.

Approaching headlights from down the road light up the street and I bend back down in my seat, hunching over as Jack parks and steps out of the car. I watch him loosen his tie as he makes his way towards the front door and snap, snap, snap away at my phone taking as many pictures as I can. It takes every part of restraint I own not to open the car door and tackle that son of a bitch into the ground.

"Make sure you get the front door, so he knows we know where he lives," Prince urges in my ear. I snap and snap again, visions of me pummelling Jack on the lawn disappearing.

I watch as he lets himself in. "I guess we should go now," I tell Prince, but he's looking past me at the house. "Wait, look."

I turn and can see right into their lounge, where Whisper is now wearing a hoodie and tracksuit bottoms, curled up on the sofa with her mum. Her mum stands and kisses Jack on the cheek before leaving the room for something, leaving Jack alone with Whisper. I find myself clenching my fists tightly as he creeps over next to her and slips an arm around her. I watch her recoil slightly, not looking him in the eye. On impulse, I snap another photo. Then I watch as his hand crawls down her front even further, and suddenly he's cupping her breast and she's frozen in time, completely unmoving. My pulse drums in my ears/

Prince says something that I don't listen to properly and then he leans over and grabs the phone from my hand and takes a bunch of photos.

After a moment Whisper pushes his hand away and stands up, stalking away. Seconds later she appears in her bedroom window, slamming the door.

"Let's go," Prince says quietly, pulling away from the curb. We ride home in silence.

I text Whisper when I get back to mine.

- **Want to visit later? I'm bored.**

Her reply comes almost instantly, and less than an hour later there's a rap at the window and I fling the curtains open as she crawls in like a little cat. "Thanks for inviting me," she whispers as she sits down on my desk chair.

"No biggie," I shrug, trying to play it all down. The relief that she's here with me and not anywhere near Jack is almost overwhelming. It makes my voice waiver a little, but I don't think she notices.

"I was gonna go to Ellie's but I've been at hers a lot recently, so it's your lucky day that I'm around," she jokes, turning the chair to face my desk and hooking her feet on one of the drawer knobs. "You know Ellie, right?"

"I know who she is. I've never spoken to her," I reply. I only know her because she's one of the only other girls in our year at school with facial piercings. I don't think she's ever even noticed I exist.

"Ah right. She's nice," Whisper tells me.

I nod, unsure where the conversation is going, and a short silence follows.

"So, what do you wanna do?" I ask eventually.

She looks around the room, chewing on her lip. "We could do some art?" she suggests, eyes landing on my sketchbooks.

"Really?"

"Yeah. I never draw. It's supposed to be relaxing, right?"

I grin. "Yeah. Let's draw." I go to my desk and get out some paper and throw a load of pen and pencil options onto the ground, and the two of us sit companionably in silence for a while, the sound of pens on paper (and scribbling on Whisper's side) the only noise.

"What are you drawing?" she asks, looking up from her own pad curiously.

"It's a secret," I tell her cryptically.

"`Mysterious," she purrs.

"Well I'll show you mine if you show me yours," I tell her with a grin.

"Cooper Nelson, are you *flirting* with me?" she gasps in mock shock. I hope it's shock and not horror, anyway.

"But yes, okay. Show me yours," she laughs.

I flip my pad around and display my picture. I've done a cartoon version of Whisper, kitted out in a striped burglar outfit climbing through my bedroom window with a menacing grin. She laughs delightedly, throwing her head back so I have to 'shh' her. "Sorry," she giggles with a whisper.

I glance to the door, but I can just hear the TV downstairs where Mum and Dad are watching something.

"That is so great," she whispers. "What am I stealing?"

My heart, I think. "My dog," I say.

"I would steal Max, to be fair," she agrees.

"Your turn, show me yours," I demand.

219

"Okay, well it's not good like yours but…" she trails off and turns her pad around. It's me. She's drawn me.

"You gave me that lovely portrait so it was only fair that I attempted to return the favour," she explains, and I might be imagining it but I feel like she's blushing.

She's drawn me face on, using a lot of straight lines that make me look manlier than I am. I'm in a t-shirt and she's coloured in my hair roughly and I'm smiling.

"Nobody's ever drawn me before," I tell her. "Thank you. I love it."

"You can keep it," she tells me, passing it over. In return, I hand over my jokey comic picture.

"Cooper!" I jump as my mum yells out, and Whisper and I look at each other, wide-eyed.

"Yes?" I shout back, gesturing to Whisper to hide. She steps behind the wardrobe and I try not to snort with laughter, her leather boots sticking out at the bottom.

"Fuck!" She whispers, looking for somewhere else.

"We're going to sleep now. See you tomorrow," Mum calls out, the sound of Dad coming up the stairs heavily.

"Okay. Night!" I shout, as Whisper kneels behind my wardrobe. I sit there on the floor, surrounded by pens, my breath held. They don't come in. They walk past straight into their own bedroom and Whisper pretends to faint in relief. I have to look away, otherwise I'm going to laugh loudly.

"You want to watch a film or something? I'm getting kind of sleepy," she says when we eventually pull ourselves together.

"Yeah. Anything in particular?" I ask, pulling my laptop over to my bed and scrolling through some options.

"Shall we watch something scary?" she says excitedly, like a child.

"Yeah, I don't mind horrors," I tell her, passing her the laptop to make a choice. She squeezes herself next to me on the bed and scrolls through, pausing to read the synopsis every now and again. Her leg is pressed right up against mine and I try not to tense, breathing slowly and deeply to try and feign casualness.

She's warm, and her jumper smells of fresh laundry. Eventually she makes her selection, picking something about a possessed doll. "Turn the lights off?" she asks, unlacing her boots.

"Sure," I reply thickly, flicking the switch and plunging us into darkness, the light from the laptop screen illuminating my bed.

I crawl back into the bed beside her and she starts the film, nestling down into the covers and leaning her entire body into mine. My arm sits awkwardly in-between us, but I'm too nervous to wrap it around her. At one particularly jumpy moment in the film she gasps, clutching at my arm and nuzzling into me.

"It's okay," I murmur, looking down at her. She's squeezed her left eye shut and is timidly peeking out of the right. It's adorable.

"Hey, Whisper. I'm really glad you're here," I tell her. "Me too," she replies, relaxing against me and eyes fixed on the screen again.

I wake up at 6am to Whisper beside me, the laptop still resting beside her and her arms splayed out above her head. She's breathing slowly and steadily, here eyelids fluttering occasionally.

I text Prince.

- Can't wait any longer. Let's drop the letter off today, straight after school. Can't stand knowing what goes on every minute we wait. Can you print the images off today??

His reply comes an hour and a half later. That time was spent drawing erratic shapes and colouring them in to keep my mind occupied, my knee jiggling the entire time.

- Sure. I already printed them off at home. Mum's got a desktop printer. Oldschool.

I almost sag in relief.

I just have to get through the day and then we can put this all behind us. I put on a red sweatshirt, grey jeans and my black trainers. My black beanie goes on too - it's cold out today. One Marmite-and-bus-ritual later and I'm at my locker avoiding eye contact with everyone in the hall.

"Hey, you!"

I turn to see Whisper at the locker beside me, leaning against it and playing a game on her phone.

"Hey," I reply. I watch her closely, looking for a sign that more bad stuff happened last night after we left, but she gives nothing away, her eyes flitting around the screen as her fingers quickly tap away at something. She slumps and groans, dropping her hand to her side. "Lost again. Dumb game." She switches her phone off.

"How was your night?" I ask. I know I'm fishing a little, but I guess curiosity is getting the better of me.

She just shrugs. "Same old. You do anything?"

I freeze for a moment, unprepared for this question. "Just saw Prince," I say. A half-truth. I'm saved by the bell for first class. "Speak later," I tell her. She doesn't even notice, already checking her timetable to work out where she's headed.

Lunchtime arrives and I sit on my own, as usual. All I can think about is seeing Prince after school and ending Jack's reign of terror. I pull out my tupperware and take a pill from my backpack, swallowing it down with water and then taking a bite of my sandwich.

I jump when the chair next to me is pulled out. Whisper sits down next to me, nonchalant as anything.

"I don't usually see you around at lunch," I comment, putting down my sad sandwich. She's usually smoking. "Happy about it, of course," I add quickly, in case I've offended her and she decides to leave.

"Yeah, I know. I kind of fancied the canteen vibe today though. It does not disappoint," she says sarcastically, scanning the room with an eyebrow raised. "Besides, Jack made me lunch for today. I have leftover pasta."

She pulls out a tupperware and I bristle at Jack's name coming out of her mouth. She comes out with it so naturally, I don't even see a hint of pain as she speaks about him. Even though she knows I know. It's all so confusing.

She stabs at her pasta with a fork and chews quickly, her face in her palm as she leans on the table, bored.

"You want to do something this weekend?" I ask. "Maybe with Prince?"

She scrutinises the tortellini speared on her fork carefully before shovelling it into her mouth and looking at the floor. "Not really sure what my future plans are yet," she says cryptically. "I'll let you know."

"Cool." I take another bite of the World's Saddest Ham Sandwich.

I still struggle with thinking of small talk to make when I'm surrounded by people, and I like that Whisper doesn't push when there's nothing to be said. I feel like everyone on the tables are staring at me, wondering why someone is finally sitting with me, what we're talking about, how stupid I sound. When I look up, nobody is looking at us. But I still feel like they are, like their eyes are burning into the back of my head and like all the chatter around us is the sound of everybody secretly laughing at me. That's why I usually sit alone at lunch, with my head down and my headphones in. It means nobody has a reason to notice me. The few times Whisper's been around for lunch I've gotten this foreign, unwelcome feeling of discomfort. Even though I know it's dumb. Nobody's looking at me. Nobody's looking at me. Nobody's looking at me.

The words repeat themselves over and over in my head through lunch and through the rest of the afternoon. I'm still saying them to myself mentally when Prince pulls up outside my house and toots his horn.

"Just running out with Prince, Mum!" I yell as I run down the stairs.

"Don't be back late. And tell him not to toot his horn like that, it's rude and disturbs the neighbours," she shouts from the kitchen.

I climb into his car and fasten my seatbelt. "Mum says to stop tooting your horn," I tell him.

"God, I love that woman," he replies as he shifts into gear.

When we arrive at Jack's office it's loud and buzzing. It wasn't like this before, but I suppose it was the end of the day last time we visited. Now it's not even 4pm.

"How do we go about this?" I ask, biting my lip.

"Okay, I'll go in because he doesn't know me and won't recognise me if there's a run-in," Prince tells me, turning around all excited. "I'll put my hat and glasses on and tell the receptionist to pass my letter on. Make out I'm a delivery courier. Hey, presto! Even if he somehow gets CCTV footage of me, he won't know who it is."

"Okay," I say, nodding along. Sounds good. And sounds safe for me, which I like. "Can I see the envelope?"

He hands it to me, and I open it. The letter is inside, and our dodgy photographs are enclosed as well, the quality a little shoddy but the content clear. I grin. This is going to work. Whisper is going to be okay. I wish I could see the bastard's face when he reads it.

"You ready?" I ask.

Prince nods and salutes me. "Aye, aye. Mission Destroy Jack is a-go." He draws a dramatic deep breath, opens the car door and gives me a final nod, his brows straight and jaw tense as he turns away from the car.

I watch him strut up to the office building with immense jealousy. He looks so calm, cool and collected. If it was me, I'd be fidgeting, sweating and probably have paused at the door for about ten minutes. He strides in confidently, speaks quickly with the receptionist, his head down. I wonder what he's saying. Is he keeping the exchange simple and unmemorable, or is he being Classic Prince and flirting with her?

Moments later and he comes back to the car, cool as a goddamn cucumber. He takes his glasses off as he approaches and winks.

He slides in, shuts the door and holds up his hands. "You can say it. I am the man." He grins, turning the car engine on.

"What happened?" I ask, staring at him.

"I just asked the receptionist to hand this to Jack when she next saw him. She said she would, so I said make sure it gets to him before end of day as it was highly important, and she assured me it would be done immediately."

"Imagine, he'll be reading it in the next hour," I say, a grin creeping onto my face.

"Mission accomplished. One slimy bastard down," Prince replies.

"We should do something to celebrate the end of this," I say thoughtfully.

"Feels weird to celebrate without Whisper," he says.

"Yeah, but she can never find out what we did. Want to get a pizza and play videogames?"

"My amigo, I can think of no better way to celebrate," Prince replies.

CHAPTER 14

THE RED MERC

We're arguing about what pizza toppings to order when my phone buzzes.

- Leave the house. Now!

My blood runs cold, and I show Prince the phone screen. "What the hell does that mean?" he asks.

"It means let's get out of here and order pizza at yours instead," I tell him decisively, whilst texting Whisper back. Why? What's happening? Will go to Prince's.

We head down the stairs and get into his car, pulling out from my driveway speedily. My hand grips my phone tightly, waiting for it to vibrate with Whisper's response.

What could have happened that I would need to leave the house?

- Are you okay? I text her again. I can see by her status that she hasn't been online in fifteen minutes, so she hasn't read any of my messages yet. What is she doing?

I chew the inside of my lip worriedly.

"What the hell?" Prince mutters. A car is heading towards him, flashing its lights excessively. Prince pulls over, slamming his break down as he's blinded by the brightness. My stomach drops. It's a red Merc.

"Prince…" I start, but before I can finish, Jack appears at his window, rapping on it with a grin plastered over his face. Prince rolls the window down, clearing his throat nervously.

"All okay?" he asks Jack with a tip of his head.

"You tell me," Jack replies, ignoring Prince and looking directly at me.

"Hello, Mr Collinden," I manage to choke out, trying to look casual.

"Cooper," he says curtly, gesturing for me to step out of the car. I gulp as I open my door, stepping out and being sure to keep the car between the two of us as he leans over the roof to speak with me. I glance at Prince, who is watching us both carefully, his knuckles white on the steering wheel and the engine still running in the background.

"Where were you after school today?" Jack asks, his voice quiet.

I swallow, and quickly throw a glance at Prince. He opens his mouth. "We were-"

"Ah," Jack holds up a hand, silencing Prince who is gazing up at him through his open window.

"I want to hear from Cooper," he says.

Clench. Unclench.

I gaze up at him defiantly. "Why do you care what I did after school?"

"Yeah, we were just hanging out," Prince says, his voice a pitch higher than usual.

"Hanging out where, exactly?" Jack asks. His eyes have darkened, and his voice is not recognisable as the man I had dinner with.

"Look, I don't know why you're coming over here, asking where I've been," I start.

He cuts me off. "Because I got an interesting package delivered at my place of work today. The thing is, I know it was a friend of Whisper's who sent it. And I'm also aware that Whisper has only three friends she has mentioned since we arrived in this town. Two of which are sat right here," he continues. "Assuming, of course, that you are Prince," he pauses to look at Prince for the first time. Prince gulps. "And I happened to drive past her third friend, Elise, on the way home from work. So I know it wasn't her stalking me at my office, delivering threats," he tells us, his voice low.

He moves to step in front of the car, closer towards me, and I instinctively step backwards. "So who else could it have been?" he asks, stepping forward again.

I shrug – or try to. It comes out as a jerky movement. I see Prince open his car door, slowly stepping out of the car so he's behind Jack, who's still edging around the front of the car and closing the gap between us.

"Maybe if you didn't do anything deserving of it, people wouldn't be leaving threats at your office," I tell him, sounding braver than I feel.

He gives a low chuckle. "You have no idea what you're talking about, kid."

I lift my chin defiantly. "I think I do."

"What's going to happen is you're going to give me whatever photographs you have. All the copies. And nobody is going to hear about this again, you understand?" I watch Prince creeping up behind him.

"I don't know what photographs you're talking about," I reply.

"Don't fuck with me, kid," he's shouting now, stepping forwards quickly. "Aargh!"

229

Prince has leapt onto his back, trying to tackle him to the ground. Jack swings like a wild gorilla and Prince goes flying onto his car bonnet, landing with a thud and groaning as he rolls off.

I run and throw a punch at Jack, but he dodges with impressive speed and clocks me around the mouth. My jaw explodes with hot pain as I stagger backwards.

"You little shits," Jack snarls, coming for me again. "Give me the damn photographs," he kicks me and I clutch at my stomach, the wind kicked out of me as I choke.

In the distance I can hear a car coming up the road and thank God that there's going to be a witness, that someone may be able to stop this. Jack steps back momentarily, even reaches a hand out to make it look like he's helping me up, but then my eyes focus on the car and the lights dim. It's Bella.

"Cooper?" she sticks her head out of her window.

"For fuck sake," Jack growls. "Get back in your car and drive away, girl."

Bella glances at me, still lying on the floor, and then at Prince who is holding onto his car for support with one hand and clutching his side with the other.

"Who the hell are you?" she asks, turning her engine off and opening her car door.

"I said, drive away," Jack roars, moving towards her. I push myself up but Prince has beaten me to it, running at Jack with a wild roar and rugby tackling him into the ground. Bella screams, staggering backwards in shock. "What are you doing Prince?"

"He's saving you," I retort, rushing forward. "Get back in the car," I yell at her.

"Cooper? What the hell? Who is he? Stop it!" she's shouting. I go to try and hold Jack's arms down but he clocks me in the jaw and I fall backwards.

"Oh my God, Cooper!" Bella screams, running forward. "That's my little brother!" she shouts, kicking Jack in the side with her pointed shoe.

Jack bellows and grabs Prince by the throat. Time seems to slow down as I watch him squeeze, Prince grasping at his neck and making small, gasping sounds. Then, Jack throws him off his chest with astounding force, Prince gasping on the road as Bella rushes forward to him.

Jack turns his attention to me. "Give me the damn photographs," he snarls, grabbing the front of my shirt and lifting me off my feet against a parked car. I scrabble to get him off me, and specks of spit are flicking into my face as he pants with rage, his eyes wide.

Suddenly a loud crack sounds and Jack drops to the ground. Bella is stood behind him, wielding Prince's heavyset binoculars. One of the lenses is now cracked. "Are you okay?" she rushes forward to me. I nod dumbly.

Prince has crawled forward and lifted Jack's head. No bleeding. His chest is rising and falling. "Let's get out of here," he croaks.

"Come back to ours," I tell him. He nods slowly. He gets into his car and drives up towards our driveway and Bella gets into her own. She looks at me.

"Just a minute," I tell her. She nods, understanding.

I watch them both drive down the street and into our driveway and I'm left with Jack, who is lying in the middle of the road.

"Bastard," I mutter, as I drag his heavy, unconscious form

out of the road and onto the pavement with a grunt. He's not light.

Then I go over to his car to shut the door, but as I do so, something catches my eye. His phone is lying on the passenger seat. On impulse I reach over and take it, before shutting the car door and running back down the street to my house.

Bella is waiting by the door. "Start talking," she says sternly, her arms folded.

The three of us are sat around the kitchen table, Bella's face ashen as we recount everything that's been happening recently. Prince is sipping from a cup of herbal tea Bella made us, looking more shaken than I've ever seen him before.

Then Mum and dad burst through the front door, making us all jump.

"We're home!" Mum sings.

"The cinema was brilliant," Dad tells us, and I can hear him taking his jacket off. Mum pokes her head around the kitchen. "Nice to see you Prince. Oh dear, what's happened to your neck?" She frowns and Prince brings a hand up to his neck, which is slowly turning blue.

Her eyes turn to me and widen. "And what happened to you? Look at you!" I haven't even looked in a mirror yet, so I don't know what damage I'm facing.

"We got jumped," Prince says quickly.

"Jumped?"

"Yeah, didn't see the guys face," Prince says.

"I found them outside and the guy had already gone," Bella adds, glancing at us.

"Well, we had best call the police," Mum says, rummaging through her handbag. "Did they steal anything?"

"No! No, Mum. Please. I really don't want to make a big deal out of this," I plead.

Dad appears in the door. "Are you sure, son?"

"Yeah, totally. It was just a dumb teenager," I beg.

"I want to hear more about this in the morning, and we will decide what to do then. As a *family*." Mum says sternly, stifling a yawn and turning to head upstairs.

I nod, grateful to have bought some more time to tie up our story.

"Did you pass a red Mercedes on the end of the road?" I ask as Dad turns to leave the kitchen.

He frowns. "No, why?"

"Just a nice new car we saw earlier," Prince says quickly.

Dad narrows his eyes at us but follows Mum up the stairs.

"Go clean yourselves up. We'll make a plan to sort all this out in the morning," Bella says, sounding more like Mum than I've ever heard before.

We're washed and I'm lying across my bed when I remember the phone with a start. "I forgot! I took his phone," I say, leaping up and going through my jacket pockets.

"You took Jack's phone?" Prince repeats from the air mattress he's lying on.

I take it out and press the home button. "Damn, it's locked," I tell him with a frustrated sigh.

"Give it here," Prince says, his hand out. A couple of minutes later the phone screen brightens and he grins. "We're in."

233

"What? How did you do that?" I ask.

"There are 5 combinations which are the most common. Jack's not a creative guy," Prince says with a smug smile. "He opted for the password 1,1,1,1," he informs me, swiping up his text messages and scrolling quickly.

"What's on it? What do you see?"

"Pretty boring. Looks like he only really messages colleagues or Whisper's mum," Prince says, sounding disappointed.

"What about his photos?"

"Just a lot of cars and boring old-people pictures," he says, sounding bored. "Woah. Hold up. I think we have something here."

"What is it?" I ask, sidling forward and craning to look at the screen as Prince's thumbs dance over the keypad quickly.

"I'm in his Drive, looking at downloads and his Cloud…" he trails off. "Oh, Jesus. Fuck." He throws the phone down.

"*What?*" I reach for the phone but he swats my hand away. "You don't want to look, man. Let's just say his Cloud folder called Holiday Snaps is *not* filled with holiday snaps. And what's in there is definitely not PG and definitely not legal."

I grimace, and watch as Prince screenshots the screen and sends a copy to his own phone, which vibrates on my desk.

"Now we really do have all the proof we need," he says.

"What's gonna happen now?" I ask quietly. "He knows where I live. What if he comes back?"

"He won't. Not when he realises his phone is missing," Prince says. He sounds so confident, I believe him.

"What about Whisper?"

There's a small silence.

"She's smart. If she told you to run, she knew he was

coming. She'll have run, too. She wouldn't have stuck around to deal with his rage," Prince says finally.

I nod, but I'm not sure I believe it. I *want* to believe it, but my head circles in scenarios where I envision him getting home, bruised and battered, beating Whisper up. I clench my hands until they feel bruised and prepare myself for a sleepless, panic-filled night.

I glance at my phone one last time before I get back into bed. Whisper never texted me back.

CHAPTER 15

PANIC

I wake up in confusion at the sound of our landline ringing. Who calls the landline?

I groan and reach over to my phone, then blink in confusion. Who is calling our house phone at 7am?

"Who the hell is that?" Prince grunts, rolling over on the air mattress. I'm too tired to reply, and just toss over. I can hear Mum on the phone in her room, but she's being very quiet. My pulse quickens. Who is calling us, and why?

There's a rap on our door a few minutes later.

"Boys, we need to chat. Come downstairs."

Never in my life have I thrown a t-shirt on and flown down the stairs so quickly, Prince on my tail.

My mum stands from the sofa, hurrying over to us, her face pale and drawn.

"Cooper," she starts, her voice strained.

"Mum? Is everything alright?" I frown at her.

"No, I'm afraid it isn't. Darling, come sit down, Prince you too. I need to tell you both something very serious," she tells us.

"Is Bella okay?" I ask immediately.

"What? Yes, God, yes, Bella is fine. Still asleep, I think. Just sit," she stammers.

Prince and I exchange a glance and sit down, my hands crossed in my lap awkwardly. "Grandma then?"

"Your granny is fine." She's wringing her hands and tugging at her sleeves, hopping from foot to foot slowly as though not sure how to stand. Eventually she runs a hand through her hair and sits down in the armchair opposite us.

"It's about your friend Whisper," she starts. Already my stomach has twisted. I feel Prince tense beside me.

"I got a call while you were out," she continues. "I'm afraid there was an… accident. She's in the hospital."

"What kind of accident?" Prince asks immediately. I'm glad he does, I can't seem to find my tongue.

Mum looks to the side and then back at us, her knuckles clicking as she kneads her hands in her lap.

"I don't want to jump to any conclusions, but they think it was some kind of overdose," she says quietly.

It's like my world stops. I can't hear anything except a strange hum, and everything seems to slow down.

"I can take you to visit her now," Mum says, standing up and heading to the coat stand.

Prince stands and I remain rooted in the spot.

I have a strange feeling in my head. One of my panics. *This is your fault, Cooper. This is all your fault.* It's my fault. I shouldn't have told her I knew, shouldn't have threatened Jack. I put too much pressure on her. I haven't been watching her closely enough. Overdose… overdose…overdose…

"It's my fault," I whisper hoarsely to Prince.

237

"It's not," he says firmly. "You've done the right thing telling me. We've sorted it out." He looks a little shell-shocked, but his voice has the confidence it always carries.

But something still isn't sitting right. All those things I said to her. I told her I couldn't stand seeing her hurting anymore. I told her she needed to sort it out. What if I pushed her too far? Jesus, I feel so sick. I start going dizzy and realise I forgot to take my meds today because I skipped lunch. I reach for my backpack and I'm scrambling around in it blindly, but I can't find them.

"Honey, do you need your meds? Shall I get you some food to take with them?" Mum's asking.

"I can't find them," I choke out.

"Dude, what do you mean you can't find them?" Prince asks. He's white as a sheet.

Suddenly a thought hits me like a freight train. A thought that makes me feel sick. It can't be... I grab my rucksack which is by my feet and begin rooting through it more manically, throwing everything aside and eventually just tipping it upside down, contents falling everywhere.

"Cooper? What are you doing?" I hear Mum say. I ignore her, scrabbling manically amongst my things like a crazy person.

But I was right.

My pills are gone. My goddamn pills are gone.

Did Whisper take them?

Did my medication almost kill the girl I think I love? I stagger backwards.

Mum rushes forward. "Cooper, what's wrong?"

Prince is stood with a grimace on his face.

Mum gets too close. "Get away from me!" I shout. I don't want her near me. I don't want anyone near me. She recoils like I've hit her.

I curl up into a ball, my hands over my head and rock slowly. I feel dizzy. I don't want to leave this spot.

"Cooper!" Mum screeches. She runs out of the room and I can hear her getting things from the kitchen cupboards but then the pounding of my pulse is all I can hear. Black spots are fading in and out of my eyes. My heart is pounding so quickly the drum in my ears has become one long buzz.

She tried to end her life. I gave her the key.

My sickness almost killed her.

I need to be alone. Alone.

Get away. Too loud, too loud, too loud. I'm covering my ears with my hands and Prince slowly places a cup of water next to me, backing away like I'm a wild animal.

Suddenly the taste of metallic fills my mouth. Dirty copper pennies. I realise I've been chewing and grinding on my inner cheek so much its bleeding. I grip my legs tighter. I want to remember what Suzie taught me but I CAN'T. THINK. CLEARLY. My brain is too

Loud

Too

Loud

Too

LOUD.

I'm sweating so much but I'm frozen. I'm so embarrassed. So ashamed. I want to get out. I want Prince to get out. I want Mum to get out. She's come back in and is spraying the vomit-soaked carpet. "Get out, get out, get out," I gasp. It's almost like a sob. I don't look up, but I hear them both leave in silence.

I rock and rock and rock. Clench, unclench, clench, unclench. Aching hands. Blood in my mouth. Blood, blood, blood. Whisper in the hospital. Did she want to die?

Did I make her want to die?

I gave her the means. I gave her what she needed to die. It's my fault. All. my. Fault.

I hear a strange strangled sound and realise it's me. I'm crying. Not even crying, sobbing and gasping and retching and screaming. Mum comes back into the room, her feet coming into my peripheral vision as I rock on the floor.

She sits across from me but doesn't try to touch me. Thank God she doesn't try to touch me. Don't touch me. Don't touch me. Don't touch me.

She starts going "shhhhhhh" again and again and again and eventually it overtakes the buzzing in my ear and the pumping in my chest and I'm still clenching and unclenching but shhhhhh and shhhhh and shhhhh.

Finally, the sweat begins to dry. I look up. It's been almost twenty minutes. I stop rocking. I unclench my fists and little black indents run across my palms.

"Do you still want to go to the hospital, to see her?" Mum asks quietly.

I manage to nod. I have to go. I can't leave her there on her own. I have to be there for her. I pick up the glass of water beside me and take a shaky sip, my stomach queasy and my mouth dry.

Prince stands awkwardly by the door, staring at his feet and the wall and everywhere other than me. I'm so embarrassed. I'm a pathetic, humiliating mess of a person.

Mum wraps me in a coat and ushers me into the car where the three of us sit in silence the entire journey.

This time when we enter the hospital, the stink of disinfectant stings my nostrils. I rub my hands up and down my jeans but they're still clammy. I look around the waiting room at all the sick people and wonder how sad someone must be to intentionally try to kill themselves when everyone else is fighting so hard to stay alive.

It makes me want to cry and I don't want to cry (again) in front of Prince so I swallow the lump in my throat and try not to gag.

"Alright boys," Mum shuffles over.

"She's in that room over there." Mum points down the poorly lit corridor where a woman is waiting on a rolling bed to be taken somewhere. She looks grey and her hand is hanging limply off the edge but she doesn't seem to care.

I see Whisper's mum down the hall. Her eyes are red and she's on the phone, pacing quickly.

"You both go ahead, I'll wait here." Mom smiles at me encouragingly and I stare blankly back. Do I want to go in? To see her?

"Come on, mate," Prince reaches out to take my arm, then pauses as if it will shock me into another attack. I don't react so he tentatively takes hold of my arm and slowly ushers me towards her room.

"I can't go in there. I don't know what I'll see," I choke out.

"Okay, okay. Tell you what, I'll go first and take a peek and let you know if I think it'll be okay," he tells me.

I don't reply, and he edges forward and peers through the glass pane on the door. He's peering through for a while and then turns to me.

"It's okay. She's awake, she looks okay."

He flaps his hand, gesturing to me to come forward as he opens the door. I take a deep breath. *3...2...1...*Suzie's voice in my head counts down.

I step into the room and look around. All around me are girls and boys, mostly teenagers but a couple of adults dotted between. A girl on one side has two huge bandages around her arms, deep brown-red stains on the inner gauge. Beside her, a younger looking girl so gaunt she looks like she may shatter, her hair limp, eyes sunken and her skin grey and pimply. A hook hangs from her bony arm, pumping a solution into her body. She looks so sad, as though she's given up on everything.

One of the adults in the room is a man, his eyes bloodshot and red rimmed as though he's cried a lot. He is staring at the ceiling blankly, his hands in fists and a monitor strapped up beside him. I've never been in a room with so many sad people.

At the end of the room as I walk down the aisle, beds either side of me filled with hopeless bodies, is Whisper.

She's sat up and pouting sulkily, but I can see she's been crying. Her eyes are watery, and her face is puffy.

"Hey," she says quietly, as though it's just another day.

"Hi," Prince says back.

I say nothing. What can I say? Sorry my meds nearly killed you?

The three of us stay awkwardly in silence, the voice of a girl crying and arguing with her parents echoing through the room.

"I'm sorry," she whispers finally.

"You took my meds," I say. My voice is scratchy.

"I know, and I'm sorry. I'm so sorry. I don't know what I was thinking." She sounds so broken.

Prince's head whips round to me. "She took your pills? Jesus, Whisper. What the hell?" He shakes his head and she looks to the floor, her lip trembling.

I clear my throat and then realise I don't really know what to say, so I don't say anything.

"Prince, can I... can I speak to Cooper alone?" Whisper asks.

I blink in surprise and Prince nods. "Sure. I'll go keep his mum company." He bows his head at me as though checking I'm okay before he leaves.

I'm left with Whisper, standing by her bed.

"I have some good news," she tells me.

"Other than that you're alive?" I say. I wince at how harshly it comes out.

She pauses for a moment, and then decides to continue. "My mum isn't here at the moment because she had to call my grandparents," she tells me.

"About you being in hospital?" I ask.

"It's Jack. He's *gone*." Her mouth tilts upwards in a little smile.

"What do you mean?" I ask, feeling a little light-headed.

"He's done a runner. She popped back earlier to get some stuff to bring in for me and he had packed up all his shit and is gone. He's gone," she says, and I look up to see she's grinning widely now, her eyes shining and voice breaking.

Despite everything, I find myself smiling back.

"Good."

"Good riddance," she nods.

I sigh and sit down at the end of her bed. "Why did you take my pills? Is that the only reason you had lunch with me? Is it because of what I said to you?" I ask. I try not to sound as goddamn pathetic as it came out, but clearly fail as she looks at me with wide, pitying eyes.

"No! No, please don't think that, Cooper. I've been sad for so long. I've been ringing suicide hotlines for ages, it was nothing to do with you! It was Him. It was just so much, knowing that you knew now. I'm so fucking ashamed. I walked over to have lunch with you and your bag pocket was open, I just saw them and took the opportunity and stole them and I'm so sorry. You need them and I abused that. I wasn't thinking, I just didn't want to be here anymore. I wanted to get away from Him, from how ashamed I am that you know, from all of this."

I nod as if I understand, even though I don't.

"You shouldn't be ashamed, though. You're the victim in this, you've done nothing wrong," I tell her. I'm trying to keep the tremor out of my voice.

"I'm just embarrassed this is happening to me, I dunno," she says quietly.

"You won't try to do it again, will you?" I ask.

She chews her lip. "They're making me go to counselling, so I guess not."

"You'll get better now that Jack's gone," I say, though it comes out sounding more like a question.

"I hope so," she says, although she sounds like she doesn't believe it herself.

"I'm glad he's gone," I tell her, and I reach over and hold her hand.

She watches me carefully. "You... you didn't have anything to do with him leaving, did you?" she asks.

I feel her eyes boring into me and force myself to look her in the eye. "Me? What could I have done?"

She nods, but her mouth tilts into a tiny smile.

Then I remember. "Whisper, you need to tell them when you go counselling, or speak to Suzie."
"Suzie?"
I nod. "About Jack. You need to tell them what's been happening and let them help you. Please?"
"Cooper, I -"
"You have to. You owe me," I cut her off. I see her hesitate, then crumble. "I swear Suzie won't tell anyone, just explain everything and that he's gone now and she can help."

She gives a drawn out sigh. "Okay. I promise. When I'm back at school I'll go see Suzie. Hey, what happened to your hand?"

She reaches over and takes my hand in hers, the palm a murky shade of purple dotted with small bloodied indents where I had clenched my fists so hard earlier.

She runs her thumb over it gently and I say nothing for a while.

Finally, I breathe in and force myself to ask the question I didn't think was appropriate for so long. "Whisper, do you want to get better?"

She chews her lip as though she doesn't know the answer, then she squeezes my hand a little tighter. "If you asked me that when I first moved here, I probably wouldn't have been able to answer. I didn't know anybody, my friends all ditched me when they found out about Jack. I felt hopeless, like it would never end. But you know what? Right now, in this moment, I really do. I want to get better. Without Jack in my future, and with you in it, I want to give being happy a real shot. I want to be happy."

I nod.

I just feel tired. So, so tired.

I sigh. Will I ever not be tired?

EPILOGUE

A GIRL CALLED WHISPER

9 Months Later

My phone buzzes. I look down. Prince.

- Meet you there at 8.30???

I fire back the thumbs up emoji, setting my phone back down on my desk.

It's Saturday, and we're going to the late-night showing of *Killathon: Two Cities Collide*, a new black comedy/horror film hybrid at the cinema. I'm actually looking forward to how goddamn awful it's going to be.

I turn back to my laptop and stretch out onto my bed, logging into my website. www.AGirlCalledWhisper.com. The first thing that pops up is the new rendition of the plastered angel I had drawn over a year ago. In this version, there are no plasters.

It all started on Whisper's birthday a few months ago, and for her present I made her this mini comic book. I spent ages illustrating it all, inking her caricature. I made her a superhero, naturally, but really witty and dry and sarcastic to match her personality. Her superpower was super strength, the story ending with her getting into a tough spot but, naturally, living to see another day. I was pretty proud of it to be honest.

Anyway, she loved it so much she cried and did that thing girls do where they flap their hands in front of their eyes a lot. And then she said she wanted me to do more, like a collection. She even scanned the front cover and framed it in her bedroom, which beats Mum's fridge door any day.

So, Prince and I were talking about it and I started my website up a couple of weeks ago and can't believe the amount of traffic it's gotten already. Prince helped me build the website and now I'm running this online zine series and all these people are reading it and commenting and following.

I scroll down through the comments page quickly before I have to leave for the cinema, soaking in the words in front of me.

Sick skills, keep them coming.

Can't wait to see what happens in the next one! Was scared for Whisper for a moment there!

What brush pen do you recommend??

I'd love to collab with you sometime, drop me a line if you're interested.

I feel like I finally have a little space where I belong, and where I can be myself completely. It feels good. Really goddamn good.

I reply to a couple of them before I realise what time it is. I need to catch the bus.

I run downstairs, grab my coat and shout, "bye, Mum!"

She calls out, "don't be back late!" and I can see her smiling as she washes the dishes through the window, chatting to my dad about something. She's gotten used to me going out on the weekends now. At first she worried constantly, but now it's almost like it's normal. I guess it *is* the new normal.

I spend the bus journey sketching plans for the next episode of my zine, and when I get off at the cinema I can already see Prince and Whisper together at the Pick 'n Mix counter, their backs to me.

"No way are gummy bears the best sweet? You're sick!" Whisper groans, shovelling chocolate buttons into her bag.

"I stand by my statement, they are the best," Prince argues, popping one into his mouth provocatively.

"Arguing already?" I ask when I'm near enough.

"Cooper! Tell Prince gummy bears are the worst of the Pick 'n' Mix options," she says, throwing Prince a pointed look before grabbing my face and kissing me on the lips. I won't ever stop loving the feeling.

She links her fingers through mine and pulls me towards the counter to pay and I shrug apologetically to Prince. "Gummy bears are the worst, to be fair."

He rolls his eyes and shakes his head as though he's mortally disappointed in me. "Bro's before hoes, dude. Bro's before hoes," he continues filling his bag. "Tell you what, you can make it up to me by hooking me up with your old pal Ellie. What do you say?" he grins at Whisper.

"For the last time, Prince. Ellie's not interested. I'm sorry." Whisper puts a hand on Prince's arm.

"Man, c'mon. She hasn't even hung out with me yet, how does she know she isn't interested?"

"I'll put in a good word," I promise Prince as he turns to continue filling his over-flowing bag of sweets.

"How was your day?" I ask Whisper, my voice lowering. I know she was going to have a difficult day at therapy today, because her therapist has been trying to convince her to tell her family about Jack. Whisper's scared they'll turn against her, but it's the first step in starting legal proceedings. She needs her family supporting her so she can get Jack locked up, where he belongs, using the phone for proof. I gave Whisper the phone and she hasn't looked at it yet, she's just not ready. But she's kept it, locked away at my house for safe-keeping and we both know that when the time comes, it's gonna be the thing that helps get justice against Jack.

"I think I'll be ready to tell my Mum about everything really soon," she admits, the slightest break in her voice.

"That's really great progress," I tell her, pushing her hand away as she hands the girl behind the counter a five-pound note and passing one from my wallet instead. I can't wait for the day Jack is rotting behind bars.

"I could have paid for that myself," she grumbles.

"Because you're a strong, independent woman. I know. But I want to treat you," I tell her.

"Fine. But I'm getting the drinks," she announces, stalking over to the bar. I grin at the back of her head.

"I don't know how you put up with her," Prince tells me, but he's smiling.

"I don't know how she puts up with me," I reply.

"Right, keep a look-out for any hot ladies. I can't keep third-wheeling you guys all the time, it's hurting my rep," Prince complains, rubbing his arm as though he's physically aching and looking around as though a beautiful single girl is going to appear, begging him to date her.

"How's the zine going?" he asks me as Whisper returns and hands me a large Coke.

"Good! I got 2,000 more hits on it today," I say.

"Amazing!" Whisper pulls me in for a hug.

"You can use it in your art school application," Prince says sensibly, eyes still scanning the room for females.

"You know what? I may just do that." I agree with a smile, wrapping my arm around Whisper's shoulders as we walk into our screen.

Clench, unclench.

ACKNOWLEDGEMENTS

I have so many people to thank for helping me continue to improve as a writer and bring this story to life, but I will keep this short and mention just a few.

My editor, Melissa Kaye, for taking my manuscript and helping to build it into what it is today.

Di Dodo Fabio for creating the beautiful artwork that decorates the cover – you helped to bring Whisper to life.

My social anxiety, for giving me the understanding Cooper needed.

My parents and Steven, for continuing to support me in everything I do.

Author Biography

C.K ROBERTSON

Callie grew up in Sussex where she often discussed The Meaning of Life with her dogs.

She now works in London, where she lives with a dog, a rabbit and a boy.

She is currently working on more books.

Keep up with her on Twitter and Instagram @ByCKRobertson

www.byckrobertson.com

Printed in Great Britain
by Amazon

78498049R00150